Y0-ABZ-772

HARLEQUIN®
Makes any time special ®

ISBN 0-373-80532-2

9 780373 805327

50425

EAN

ISLAND ROMANCES

HARLEQUIN

COLLECTOR'S
EDITION

Seduced by the Enemy

KATHRYN ROSS

"You are a very beautiful woman, Helena, and I'd very much like to make love to you."

Helena swallowed hard and tried to find her voice, but it seemed to have deserted her.

Tate's hand moved from her throat down over the smooth bareness of her shoulder. "Do you hear me, Helena? I want you...I know you want me." He moved closer; she could feel his breath against her heated skin. "Tell me you want me...."

"I..." She tried to deny him...she tried desperately to speak...but her voice wouldn't function. Her heart felt like a wild caged creature inside her as his lips came closer to hers. She moistened their dryness, heat and sudden longing sweeping through her in a wild, sweet rush. "Yes." She breathed the word into the tropical heat of the night. It was just a whisper of intense longing. "Yes..."

KATHRYN ROSS was born in Zambia, where her parents happened to live at that time. Educated in Ireland and England, she now lives in a village near Blackpool, in England. Kathryn is a professional beauty therapist, but writing is her first love. As a child she wrote adventure stories, and at thirteen was editor of her school magazine. Happily, ten writing years later *Designed with Love* was accepted by Harlequin. A romantic Sagittarian, she loves traveling to exotic locations.

Seduced by the Enemy

KATHRYN ROSS

ISLAND ROMANCES

HARLEQUIN®

TORONTO • NEW YORK • LONDON
AMSTERDAM • PARIS • SYDNEY • HAMBURG
STOCKHOLM • ATHENS • TOKYO • MILAN • MADRID
PRAGUE • WARSAW • BUDAPEST • AUCKLAND

ISBN 0-373-80532-2

SEDUCED BY THE ENEMY

First North American Publication 2002.

Visit us at www.eHarlequin.com

Printed in U.S.A.

CHAPTER ONE

STEPPING off the plane into the hot shimmering sunshine of Barbados was like stepping from a black and white photograph back into colour. Drab grey London felt like another planet away.

Helena felt a tug on her heartstrings. She loved this island, she was relieved to be home...and yet there was a murmur of disquiet as she remembered how she had felt when she had flown out of here five years ago.

Briskly she tried to dismiss the shadows of remembrance and headed off to collect her luggage. The past was forgotten; all that mattered now was sorting out her father's problems.

She could still hardly believe that her father had managed to get himself into such a financial mess. Lawrence Beaumont had always been a very shrewd businessman. Helena's heart thudded nervously as she remembered the phone call from Paul last week. It had been that call which had panicked Helena into booking the first available flight home. She had never heard her brother so worried—he was usually so calm, so laid-back.

She picked up her suitcase and headed quickly for Immigration. The formalities didn't take long, and once through the barriers she scoured the crowds anxiously, looking for her brother's friendly smiling face. There was no sign of him anywhere. She frowned and glanced at her watch. He was late—not a fact that should have surprised her when she thought about it.

Her eyes searched around the airport again, and it was then that she noticed a familiar figure striding confidently through the crowds. Her heart lurched with surprise. The figure was tall and undeniably handsome—she recognised Tate Ainsley immediately.

He was wearing a tropically light business suit, which looked expensive and very stylish on his broad-shouldered frame. His hair was still jet-dark, despite the fact that he must be in his late thirties now.

What on earth was he doing here? she wondered frantically. It was six years ago now since her father had married Tate's sister Vivian. While Helena liked Vivian…Tate was an entirely different proposition. She had always felt uneasy around the man, and if what her brother had told her on the phone was true then her mistrust of him was well-founded.

Her apprehension soared as he looked around and then started to move in her direction. There was no doubt that he was walking towards her as vivid blue eyes the colour of the Caribbean Sea sliced directly into hers. 'Hello, Helena.' His voice, deep and attractive, made a few women nearby glance over at him with interest.

'Tate! I'm surprised to see you here.' Her voice was slightly strained as she strove to be coolly polite.

'Not half as surprised as I was to hear you were coming home.' His eyes flickered briefly over her long dark hair which was pulled severely back from her creamy skin, emphasising the lovely bone structure of her face and the striking green eyes.

So he had heard that she was coming home! It was surprising how news travelled so quickly on this island;

she had only faxed her father a couple of days ago with the news. She wondered how many other people knew she was here…she wondered if Cass knew…

Immediately the thought flickered into her mind she swept it aside angrily. She didn't want to think about him…if she started to think about him she might run back through the doors behind her straight onto the first available plane to London.

'How long are you here for?' Tate asked now.

She shrugged, unwilling to divulge anything much to this man until she found out the exact circumstances at home. 'Long enough to be of some help to my father.' She fixed him with a rather pointed look. 'I gather there have been a few problems at home?'

'A few problems' was putting it mildly. Paul had been beside himself with fear when they had spoken. Apparently bad investments…bad management…had put the Beaumont estate in a state of near ruin. And according to Paul it was all this man's fault.

If it was Tate's fault he certainly didn't look worried. He just grinned. 'Nothing we can't handle.'

Anger bristled through her at the arrogance of such an answer. Paul had told her in no uncertain terms that the situation was serious. Obviously Tate didn't want her to realise this…it was probably in his best interests to keep a cool façade.

'Well, I suppose the figures will speak for themselves, won't they, Tate?' Her tone was brisk and businesslike. Let him stew on that, she thought, with a gleam of satisfaction. She was nobody's fool, and she wasn't going to be palmed off with glib comments.

'I suppose they will.' He sounded most unconcerned, as if he found her frostiness merely amusing. His lips twisted in a half-smile that lit up his rugged features.

He was too attractive, she thought warily. Of course, he was not her type. There was a ruthless look about him—a light of harsh determination in his sea-blue eyes. It wasn't hard to remember who his ancestors had been...what they had been. Her gaze fell on the jagged scar that ran down the side of his face and she shivered involuntarily.

'Well, it's been nice bumping into you, Tate, but I really must dash.' She glanced pointedly at her watch. What she wanted was to get home—the sooner she found out exactly what was going on, the sooner she could start to take Tate Ainsley down a peg or two. 'I'm supposed to be meeting someone—'

'I know.' His smile widened even further. 'That someone is me.'

She frowned, totally perplexed. 'But Paul promised to pick me up from the airport—'

'Paul couldn't make it. Your father asked me to come.'

'I see.' This piece of news totally astounded Helena. She had thought Paul would be here come hell or high water.

'Well, it's really very kind of you to put yourself out like this.' She didn't know what else to say—she was totally confused by this turn of events. Paul had told her that Tate Ainsley was the enemy, that he was out to ruin their father, so why was he allowing the man to pick her up like this? Why wasn't he here, filling her in on events?

'It's my pleasure.' His voice echoed the dry amusement in his eyes. 'After all, we are practically family.'

'Hardly,' Helena muttered swiftly. Was that the angle Tate was playing with her father? she wondered grimly. Was he giving him dodgy financial advice under the guise of being a concerned member of the family?

Helena found it hard to believe that her father could have been so naïve as to be taken in by such sentiments. In the past Lawrence had always treated Tate with suspicion. Yet the fact that he had asked Tate to pick her up pointed towards how friendly he must now be with the man. It was all very puzzling.

'So where is Paul anyway?' There was a hint of brisk annoyance in her tone that she tried very hard to disguise.

Tate shrugged. 'No idea... Probably with some blonde bombshell, if I know your brother.'

Helena glared at him, her green eyes glimmering deep emerald. Much as she had to admit deep down that this could very well be true, she was far too loyal to let it pass without standing up for her young brother.

'It's five years since I've seen Paul—I'm sure he would have been here if it was at all possible.'

'If you say so.' Tate picked up her bag, his attitude one of insouciant unconcern.

He headed for the exit, and Helena followed him with a feeling of reluctance. Just what was going on? she wondered nervously. Where on earth was her brother?

Paul was not renowned for being reliable. He was a tennis coach with a lot of skill, and he was also something of a ladies' man. If a pretty young girl fluttered her eyelashes at him he was capable of forgetting what day it was, let alone that his sister was waiting to be picked up. Yet she didn't think that was the reason why he hadn't turned up today. His tone had been far too serious when they had spoken on the phone.

He had been the one who had insisted that he collect

her when she had mentioned getting a taxi. He had said that he wanted to talk with her before she saw their father, that there were a lot of facts he wanted to arm her with first. What were the facts? she wondered for the millionth time. Apprehension knotted tight in her stomach.

The sunshine was blinding outside, the heat overwhelming. Tate led the way with long strides to where a very expensive Mercedes convertible was illegally parked on double yellow lines.

Helena's mouth set in a firm line as she noticed this fact. Was Tate a man with little regard for authority? Did he think that because he was wealthy and powerful he was above the law?

'You're lucky you didn't get a ticket,' she said grimly as he opened the boot of the car and put her case in.

'They allow you a few minutes to pick up from here, and your flight was exactly on time.'

'In London you would have been clamped.'

He grimaced. 'It's no wonder you look stressed…living in London must be hell.'

He said the words with a teasing light in his eyes, and despite herself she had to smile.

'Welcome home to sunny, laid-back Barbados.' He reached out a hand and touched the smooth curve of her cheek in a gesture that made an instant flow of angry reaction flow through her body. 'Is it really five years since you left?'

With complete disregard for the fact that her expression was now one of extreme displeasure, his gaze moved over her in a more leisurely appraisal. He took in the slender curves of her body, the classically elegant blue suit.

'You've certainly changed,' he murmured contemplatively. 'What happened to the young skinny schoolgirl who left?'

'Don't be ridiculous,' she snapped with agitated impatience. 'I was nineteen when I left—hardly a schoolgirl.'

He shrugged. 'You've grown up, though…London has given you a very sophisticated air.'

It was true that London had given her a certain polish. The naïve and fresh-faced young woman who had left Barbados had blossomed into a successful career woman.

'What do you do for a living these days?' he asked nonchalantly as he opened the car door for her.

'I'm a financial adviser with a leading bank.' She met his blue gaze directly, trying to see if there was a flicker of unease in them. 'I go through people's accounts, and if there are any discrepancies, any problems, I always find them.'

She spoke the words succinctly—she wanted this man to know that she was a professional and damned good at her job. She wanted to wipe the look of complacency from those handsome features.

'Really?' He didn't look in the slightest bit perturbed—in fact, he looked vaguely amused.

'Have I said something funny?' She frowned with annoyance.

'Not at all.' He watched as she settled herself in the comfortable leather seat, his gaze flicking briefly over her long legs. 'It's just that you don't look like any financial adviser I've ever met!' He closed the door on her before she had a chance to reply to that.

She watched in brooding silence as he walked

around towards the driver's side of the car. That was the kind of chauvinistic remark she would have expected from Tate Ainsley. He was a tough kind of man…a man's man, with a hard edge. In those respects he was probably a bit like her father—Lawrence also was the type who thought that women had no place in the world of finance.

'So what exactly is it that brings you back to Barbados?' Tate enquired casually as he got into the seat next to her and started up the engine.

Helena hesitated. She didn't know what this man was up to, and until she did she needed to choose her words carefully. 'I was overdue for a visit,' she answered simply. 'And when Paul mentioned my father's money problems I thought it was best if I came right away.'

'So Paul's been filling you in, has he?' There was a note of mockery in Tate's voice now that didn't escape Helena's attention. Before she could say anything, however, Tate went on more seriously, 'Has he told you that Lawrence hasn't been well?'

Helena's heart skipped a beat anxiously. 'No…no, he hasn't.' She shot a worried look at him. 'What's wrong with him?'

'It's nothing to worry about,' Tate said soothingly. 'He's just tired and a bit stressed out.'

'About what, exactly?' Helena demanded, a hard edge to her tone. By the sounds of things she hadn't returned a moment too soon. Why hadn't Paul mentioned anything about her father's health?

'Just overwork,' Tate said lightly. 'Vivian asked me to warn you. She's anxious that nobody upsets him in any way.'

Helena frowned. 'I certainly have no intention of

upsetting my father.' Her voice rose sharply. Who did this man think he was anyway?

'No, of course not.' Tate's voice was calm. 'It's just that he's very touchy at the moment. You know Lawrence—can't stand for anyone to tell him he's over-doing things. He flew off the handle when the doctor suggested that he should take a vacation. And I believe he had words with Paul last week over something and nothing.'

'Oh, yes, I've heard about that.' Helena was quick to intercede. She wanted Tate to know that she was well aware of why Paul and her father had had words.

Something and nothing, indeed! Her brother had told her exactly what had happened, and the argument had all been due to Tate. Apparently Paul had told his father straight that Tate was leading him financially astray, and to Paul's astonishment Lawrence had taken extreme exception to the remarks.

'I don't think it was over something trivial, though.' Helena turned accusing eyes towards Tate. 'I rather thought that it was over the fact that Pop has been taking some bad advice.'

Tate slanted a glance towards her, but instead of looking worried he merely shrugged. 'I haven't a clue what they argued about. But, as I said, your father is suffering from the effects of stress and overwork. I've been trying to take some of the strain off him by sending over one of my secretaries to give him a hand.' He shook his head. 'But Lawrence is a stubborn fellow who doesn't easily accept help.'

Helena was startled by this statement. Tate sounded as if he was genuinely concerned about her father. His words certainly didn't sound like those of a man who would deliberately give misleading advice to wreck her father's finances. But then Tate was probably a very cunning man, she reminded herself sharply.

She ran contemplative green eyes over the man beside her. She knew that Tate was ambitious and determined, and that he had a reputation for being a hardheaded businessman. According to Paul, Tate had been phenomenally successful in the five years since she had been away, but due to over-extending himself with over-ambitious plans he was suffering severe financial losses…losses he was making up by duping her father.

'Well, it's just as well I've come home,' she answered him coolly. 'I'm very experienced with financial problems. I'll be able to help out—go through Pop's accounts with a fine-tooth comb.'

'I'm sure Lawrence will be very relieved.'

She glanced across and met his blue eyes head-on; there was a laughing gleam in them that made her temper rise sharply. 'I can assure you that if there are any problems…any discrepancies in my father's accounts, I will be able to find them,' she told him in no uncertain tone.

'Oh, I'm sure you will.' He shook his head, the amusement on his handsome features not dying for a moment. 'It's just that knowing Lawrence as I do, I'm sure you'll have your work cut out getting him to even open his accounts for you.'

Her hands curled into tight fists in her lap. So now she knew why Tate was so unconcerned by her comments. He was aware of her father's outlook on women in the workplace and was obviously banking on the fact that she would get nowhere near her father's books.

'Oh, he'll open them for me.' Somehow she managed to inject far more confidence into her tone than she was feeling.

'Lawrence will be disappointed when you start trying to talk business with him,' Tate reflected as he turned the car down quiet country lanes, through rolling green countryside. 'He's under the impression that you're coming home to tell him that you're getting married.'

Her eyes widened in complete astonishment at that statement. She hadn't told her father the real reason for this visit for the simple reason that she knew it would have annoyed him. Lawrence was a proud man, and he would have been severely embarrassed if he'd thought that Helena was coming home because Paul had told her that he was in a financial mess. But why he should think that she was getting married completely baffled her.

'What on earth has given him that idea?' she murmured, with a perplexed shake of her head.

'Might have something to do with the fact that you haven't visited in five years and now you are suddenly descending out of the blue with very little warning.'

Helena frowned. Was it her imagination, or was there a note of censure in his tone? 'I haven't been home because I haven't been able to get sufficient time off work,' she said stiffly. This wasn't true, but she was damned if she was going to start delving into her personal life to answer his nosy questions.

'So your reasons for not coming home before now are nothing to do with Cass?'

The outrageously personal question took her breath away. 'Certainly not!' It was appalling how the mere mention of Cass's name could send a sharp frisson of electricity through her body. That man had hurt her so much that it was painful just to think of him. 'I—I don't even know what you mean by that statement,' she muttered nervously.

He laughed at that. 'Come on, Helena, I saw you crying your eyes out over him...remember?'

Helena's heart thudded wildly at the reminder of such a distressing moment. With difficulty she closed her mind on the memory and summoned an air of indifference. 'That's all a very long time ago. I'd forgotten about it until you mentioned it.'

'Oh, I see.' The amusement in his tone very nearly threatened to snap her composure. At that moment she would dearly have loved to tell him to go to hell.

'So is there someone else?' he continued on casually.

With great difficulty she refrained from telling him to mind his own business. 'I'm not coming home to tell Pop that I'm getting married,' she said stiffly. 'Does that answer your question?'

'Not really.' He grinned. 'But it will do for now.'

He turned the car through the gateway to her home, distracting her thoughts. Her eyes moved eagerly over the fields of sugar cane shimmering in the heat of the sun. She had dreamt of this moment for five long years. This was the place dearest to her heart, the place where she had grown up. She had missed it terribly.

When the large plantation house came into sight through the tall palm trees, she felt like crying for a moment. Memories of childhood stirred deep inside— memories of her mother, of happy days.

'Glad to be back?'

Tate's voice made her try to pull her emotions tightly in check. She nodded. 'And relieved that it looks just the same as I remembered it.'

Tate pursed his lips. 'Nothing stays the same forever.'

She frowned, wondering what he meant by that. 'This house has remained relatively unchanged for generations.'

'That's not strictly true. Beaumont House used to receive all its income from sugar—jut as the Ainsley estate did. Now the sugar trade has declined and the plantations have turned towards other investments.'

'I hardly need a lesson in the economy of the island, Tate,' she told him crisply. 'I'm well aware that the sugar trade has declined.'

'Then you know that there have been big changes on estates like Beaumont,' he pointed out calmly.

'I know my father has diversified—he did that a long time ago.' She looked at him sharply. Was he making excuses? Was he trying to tell her that her father's problems were down to the economic climate, not to mishandling? He was cool, she had to give him that. Just what game was Tate Ainsley playing? she wondered cautiously.

'Up until now he has done very well from his investments,' she continued succinctly. 'I sincerely hope that he hasn't changed his business tactics.' She couldn't resist the dig. She knew damn well that her father had changed his tactics to suit Tate...with disastrous consequences. Let him try and explain himself out of that.

Tate merely laughed. 'There speaks a true banker. "Play it safe" being the banking war cry. Let me tell you that remaining static in this economic climate is like trying to tread water in a hurricane. You have to move boldly forward with the times if you want success.'

Green eyes collided directly with his deep blue gaze. She didn't care for his mocking tone. 'Bold' was a word that seemed to sit well on Tate Ainsley's shoulders. She was willing to bet that he took some very unorthodox risks in business. 'You can only move boldly forward if you have the means and the safety nets in place to do so,' she told him pointedly.

He smiled at that. 'Well, you would say that. I rest my case—you're a member of the ''play it safe'' brigade.'

'And what way do you play, Tate?' she asked directly, an edge of incrimination in her tone.

'Have dinner with me tomorrow night and we can discuss strategy if you like,' he offered casually, completely unruffled by her tone.

The invitation caught her off balance, as did the gleam of taunting mirth in his deep eyes. Was he deliberately baiting her? she wondered with annoyance, because he seemed to be enjoying putting her on the spot.

'I don't think there would be much point in us discussing business strategy,' she told him calmly. 'Comparing your ideas and mine would be like comparing a fox's idea of how to survive the winter with a squirrel's.'

He laughed at that. It was a genuine, warm sound in the sweetly fragrant air. 'I take it I'm the fox?'

'What do you think?' She grated drily, meeting his blue eyes with a look that told him most definitely that he was.

Yet underneath her stiff, instinctive antagonism to his approaches in business she had to admit in that instant to finding something very appealing about the roguish gleam in Tate Ainsley's eye... The idea was fleeting and ludicrous, and she instantly dismissed it with severe anger. What was the matter with her? she wondered furiously. Hadn't she learnt her lesson where men like Tate Ainsley were concerned?

She was extremely relieved when Tate pulled the car to a halt outside the house, putting an end to their conversation. As soon as the car engine stopped, the front door of the house opened and her father came out onto the wooden veranda, closely followed by Vivian. Hurriedly Helena reached for the doorhandle and stepped out to run towards him.

'Helena, thank heavens you are home.' Lawrence Beaumont came down the steps, and she was embraced in strong arms and held tightly.

She closed her eyes and clung to him. 'It's good to be home, Pop. I can't tell you how good.'

It was a few moments before she had gathered her emotions together enough to pull away and look at her father calmly. He didn't seem any different. A little tired, perhaps, and there was a drawn look about his face that hadn't been there before.

Lawrence was now in his early sixties, but he still had a rugged attractiveness. His sandy-blond hair was still thick, and his body powerfully built.

'You've hardly changed.' Helena smiled through a glimmer of tears.

'Well, that's more than we can say about you,' Vivian put in as she came down to join them.

Helena turned with a smile and reached to kiss her stepmother.

'You look fabulous,' Vivian said truthfully as they broke apart.

'So do you.' Helena's eyes moved wistfully over the other woman. Vivian was wearing a speedwell-blue summer dress that emphasised her superb figure. Her skin was pale and she had smouldering red lips and dark eyes. Her hair was a soft, natural blonde.

Vivian was just thirty-three years of age—it was six years since she had given up her modelling career to marry Helena's father, but her looks certainly hadn't diminished. If anything she was more beautiful now than she had been before.

'Thanks for collecting Helena.' Lawrence went to give Tate a hand with her luggage, but he waved him away.

'I can manage,' he said, smiling. 'Your daughter travels light.'

'I hope that's not an indication of how long you'll be staying?' Lawrence asked, turning anxious eyes onto Helena.

'Give me a chance to unpack before I start talking about leaving,' Helena prevaricated with a smile.

Her father nodded, and together they moved into the house.

Overhead fans made a soft whirring sound and sent a delicious waft of air over Helena's heated skin as she stepped into the wide hallway. The doors through to the lounge were open, and her eyes moved over the soft gold furnishings with delight. Everything was exactly as it had been when she had left.

The house was furnished almost exclusively with antiques, and stepping through the doorway was like stepping back in time to the colonial era. The floors were polished wood, and they creaked underfoot like a ship's galley. Crystal lights made a soft tinkling sound in the gentle breeze from the fans.

'Leave Helena's luggage by the staircase, Tate,' Lawrence said briskly as he moved into the lounge. 'Come through and join us for a drink of champagne.'

'Champagne?' Helena watched as her father marched to where an ice-bucket and glasses had been left ready and waiting for them. Champagne hardly fitted in with the picture her brother had painted of financial troubles.

'Tate very kindly brought it over earlier, ready for your homecoming.'

'I see.' Helena didn't really see at all. Why on earth should Tate bring champagne over to welcome her home?

She glanced across and met his deep blue gaze. He was watching her, a strange, almost hooded expression in his eyes. Whatever his reasons, Helena thought in that instant, she doubted they had anything to do with generosity.

She watched as her father poured out five sparkling glasses of the frothy liquid. 'Is Paul joining us?' she asked hopefully.

There was a moment's awkward silence. 'I've told your brother not to come here until he gets a civil tongue in his head,' Lawrence said in a gruff tone.

Helena's heart sank. The argument between Paul and her father had obviously been even worse than she had thought. She had hoped that they might have patched things up for her homecoming.

'The other glass is for Mary,' Vivian put in swiftly. 'She's been so excited about your return; she's been dashing around all day, fussing and flapping to make everything perfect.'

'She's done everything bar kill the fatted calf,' Tate added, a hint of dry amusement in his tone.

Was that a dig implying that she was the errant stray daughter, finally back to the fold? Helena glanced over at him, wondering again at his motivations.

'Ah, here's Mary now,' Vivian said with a smile as the door swung open and a plump black woman came rushing into the room.

'Oh, Miss Helena, you're home!' Mary's voice was filled with excitement. 'I didn't hear the car...and I've been listening out for it for what seems like hours.'

'Mary, it's so good to see you.' Helena smiled and went to embrace the woman who had been more than just a housekeeper at Beaumont House over the years.

When Helena's mother had died Mary had been a close friend to Helena. She had comforted the grief-stricken nine-year-old and had taken over the running of the house, becoming a mother substitute to both her and Paul when Lawrence Beaumont had been unable to cope with his own feelings of grief, let alone his children.

'Let me look at you.' Mary's round face beamed with good nature as she stepped back from her. 'My Lord, you look as pretty as a picture.'

'Doesn't she just?' Much to Helena's embarrassment, Tate was the one to agree with this statement. He lifted the champagne glasses and handed one each to Helena and Mary. 'I'd like to propose a toast,' he said, holding Helena's gaze with steady blue eyes. 'Welcome home, Helena. May your visit be a long and memorable one.'

Helena had a feeling it was going to be more than just memorable. She had a very strong feeling that it was going to be unforgettable.

'Hear, hear.' Lawrence topped the glasses up once they had taken a few sips of the golden liquid.

The sound of the telephone ringing made Mary put down her glass and hurry from the room.

'Will you stay and have some dinner with us Tate?' Lawrence asked.

Helena noted that her father's voice wasn't just polite—he sounded as if he genuinely would have welcomed the other man's company.

Tate glanced at his watch. 'I'd love to, but I've got an important meeting in an hour. I really should be leaving now.'

About time, Helena thought grimly. It should be Paul joining them for dinner, not Tate Ainsley. What on earth was her father thinking of?

Lawrence nodded, obviously disappointed. Then he turned his attention towards his daughter. 'So, Helena,' he said bluntly, 'put me out of my misery. Have you come home to tell us you're getting married?'

Helena tried very hard not to blush. So Tate had been right! He seemed to be very much privy to her father's personal thoughts, she observed with concern.

'No, Pop,' she said with a shake of her head. 'I've come back to see you—there's nothing more to it than that.'

'Thank heavens for that,' Lawrence said fervently. 'Not that I don't want you to get married—on the contrary, I think it's high time you tied the knot and gave me some grandchildren to bounce on my knee—but I don't want you marrying somebody miles away in London... I want you to marry someone closer to home.' Her father's voice was heavy with implication.

Helena felt sure that her face was crimson as she met Tate's coolly amused glance.

She pulled her eyes away from him, angered by his air of arrogant amusement. 'Sorry to disappoint you, Pop,' she finally managed to say in a tightly controlled voice, 'but I'm married to my work. I'm a career girl.'

Lawrence shook his head, looking totally disgusted with such a statement.

She was extremely relieved when they were interrupted by Mary coming back into the room. 'Phone for you, Miss Helena,' she said cheerfully. 'It's your brother.'

'You can take it in my office,' Lawrence said grimly, his very tone of voice conveying how displeased he was with Paul.

Helena put down her champagne and hurried towards the hall. She was extremely anxious to talk to Paul. Perhaps now he could shed some light on the exact situation here.

Her father's study was a room Helena had always felt comfortable in. The walls were lined with books and Lawrence's huge desk looked out over splendid gardens which were ablaze with tropical colour. She perched on the edge of the desk, but her eyes were barely taking in the view outside—all her thoughts were centred on Paul at the other end of the line.

'Sorry I didn't make the airport. Vivian rang me this morning and said that Pop wanted Tate to pick you up.' His voice was low, and he sounded utterly depressed.

'What's going on, Paul?' Helena asked gently. 'Pop seems to be very angry with you…more than I ever could have imagined.'

'Well, I told you.' Paul's voice was aggrieved now. 'It's that Ainsley fellow, poisoning his mind. I suppose he's still there?'

'Drinking some champagne that he brought over,' Helena informed him wryly.

'Hell, the man has nerve. Over a million down the drain, and he's got Pop—'

'A million what...dollars?' Helena's heart missed a beat. 'I don't follow this at all, Paul.'

'If you want it bluntly, Tate has talked Pop into investing all that money into buying shares in an emerald mine.'

'An emerald mine?' Helena wondered if her brother was kidding for a second. It was like some kind of joke.

'Ridiculous, isn't it?' Paul grated heavily. 'The biggest laugh is that Pop invested the money ages ago and he hasn't had a bean—or should I say a gem?—in return for it yet. But still he refuses to believe he's being duped...the man is totally convinced that it's a great business opportunity.'

'But where did he get all that money to invest?' Helena asked, totally bemused. She knew for a fact that her father hadn't got that kind of cash to play with.

'He's sold nearly everything—all his other business investments, and that prime piece of land by Bounty Bay.'

Helena felt suddenly heartsick. That land had belonged to her mother's family...it had been in the family for generations and was of great sentimental value.

'Who did he sell to?' Almost before she asked the question she knew the answer.

'Who do you think?' Paul spat out venomously. 'Tate Ainsley, of course. He's wanted that land for years, and he got it for a song compared to what it was worth. I could have got twice as much money from another buyer who told me he was very interested.'

Through the open window Helena could see Tate and Vivian walking towards his car. Tate was laughing at something the other woman was saying. He looked tremendously handsome—the sun was glinting off his jet-black hair and he had a laid-back, devil-may-care look about him.

So, well he might laugh, Helena thought contemptuously. Obviously he thought he had the Beaumont household exactly where he wanted it.

Her mouth set in a firmly determined line. No wonder Tate was working so hard to keep in her father's good books—no wonder he was bringing over champagne and acting as if he cared about Lawrence's health. He was probably hoping that if he hung on a little longer he would acquire Beaumont House for a knock-down price, the way he had acquired everything else.

'He hasn't been turning his particular brand of charm on you, has he, Helena?' her brother asked anxiously. 'You aren't fooled by him, are you?'

'Of course not,' she told him in a strong voice. 'I've got Tate's measure now, and I can assure you that he's not going to get away with fooling anyone for very much longer.'

CHAPTER TWO

HELENA couldn't sleep that night. Thoughts of Tate
Ainsley and worries about her father whirled inces-
santly in her mind. As soon as the first rays of sunlight
slanted through her bedroom window she got up and
went downstairs to make herself an early-morning cup
of tea.

She was moving silently across the hallway when a
sound from her father's study stopped her in mid-track.
Surely her father wasn't working at this hour? With a
frown she went to investigate.

Lawrence Beaumont was seated behind his desk,
wading his way through a pile of paperwork.

'Pop, you're supposed to be taking things easy!' she
said with dismay.

'Good morning.' He looked up and smiled at her,
completely undeterred. 'I am taking things easy. You
know the old adage—"early to bed, early to rise"…?'

Lawrence had retired to his study soon after dinner
last night, and it had been midnight when she had heard
him coming up to bed. However, she refrained from
saying so. Instead she erred on the side of diplomacy
and said, 'You're working too hard.'

'And you've been talking to Vivian.'

She had been talking to Vivian last night. Her stepmother was extremely concerned that Lawrence
wouldn't slow down.

'Who has been talking to your doctor.'

'Lot of nonsense.' Lawrence waved his hand scornfully.

Helena came further into the room, closing the door behind her. She was wearing a tennis skirt and a short white T-shirt. 'You and Viv having a game this morning?' Lawrence asked conversationally. Helena knew it was his attempt to change the subject.

She nodded. 'In about half an hour—before the sun gets too hot.' She looked at him more pointedly. 'It was going to be an early-morning ride, but Vivian tells me you've sold the horses.'

Lawrence looked a little uncomfortable. 'Yes, well…Tate made me a good offer.'

Helena very much doubted that. She sighed and sank down in the chair opposite to him. 'Why didn't you tell me, Pop? All the times I have phoned, and you've never said a word.'

Lawrence looked at her blankly.

'Your financial problems.' Helena's voice was gentle now. 'You should have told me. I can help.'

'Everything is under control,' Lawrence muttered quickly. 'No need for you to worry. No need at all.'

'But, Pop, Paul says—'

'Has Paul been filling your head with nonsense?' Lawrence's tone grew suddenly angry, and his face started to redden.

Conscious of his health, Helena tried to defuse the situation and calm him down. 'He just suggested that you had a few problems, that's all.'

'Knowing Paul, I'm sure he didn't stop there.' Her father leaned across the desk. 'I hope you haven't repeated anything he has said? It would break Vivian's heart to hear the scurrilous comments that boy has made.'

'No, of course not.' Helena shook her head. She had no intention of upsetting Vivian—she knew how much the woman loved her brother. She had, however, tried to ask her stepmother about the financial difficulties they were in, but it had soon become clear that Vivian didn't know anything about the business.

'Look, Pop.' She dropped her voice to a reasonable tone. 'Paul just said you were having a few difficulties, and I thought that I could go through your books and help you out. After all, I am—'

'Thanks for the offer, Helena, but everything is under control.'

'But I can—'

'Helena, I don't want to hear another word.' Lawrence's tone was ominous. He leaned back in his chair and glanced at his watch. 'Tate is sending his secretary over this morning anyway. So I've got all the help I need.'

Apprehension darted through her at those words. Why was Tate going to that trouble? Was his secretary his spy in the camp? 'I suppose Tate will be coming over as well?' she asked carefully, then couldn't help adding, 'You never used to trust him.'

'That was before I really knew him.' Lawrence met her eyes firmly. 'Tate Ainsley is a fine man.'

Unless she could prove otherwise, there was nothing more to be said. Helena stared at her father, feeling helpless and frustrated. There were a million things she would have liked to say at that juncture, but she didn't dare for fear of raising his blood pressure. It was obvious that he wasn't going to let her help him. He was just so damned stubborn.

But what could she do? She couldn't let Tate Ainsley win—she couldn't just stand by and watch him ruin everything her father had worked so hard for.

'What time are you expecting him?' she asked coolly. Her choice was clear. She couldn't risk upsetting her father…but Tate was an entirely different matter.

Helena didn't linger after her tennis match with Vivian. She headed straight around the side of the house, intending to shower and change and be back in her father's office before Tate arrived. She came to an abrupt halt at the sight of Tate's car parked on the drive.

He was standing on the front steps, deep in conversation with a young woman who was dressed very stylishly in a buttercup-yellow suit, her long blonde hair arranged fashionably around a perfectly made-up face. Helena recognised the girl immediately.

Antonia Summers had been in her class at school. She hadn't been a very popular girl, and Helena remembered vaguely that she had been an incredibly jealous type. Of course, that had been a long time ago, and the girl had probably changed a lot since then. Helena also remembered that Antonia had once had an almighty crush on Tate.

They both looked over towards her as she moved forward. 'Good morning, Helena.' Tate's eyes swept over her, encompassing her short white skirt and the cropped T-shirt with one sweep of his eyes.

Helena cursed the fact that she was so scantily clad. She hadn't even done her hair this morning; it was scraped back out of the way in a ponytail.

'I think you know Antonia, my secretary, don't you?' he continued smoothly.

So the girl was now working for Tate…what a small old world, Helena thought drily. She smiled politely and said hello.

'Been playing tennis?' Tate asked nonchalantly.

Helena nodded. It took all her inner strength just to be civil to this man. 'I was going to go riding,' she muttered with rancour, 'except that Pop has given away the horses.'

'I've bought them,' Tate corrected her with equanimity. 'But don't worry, they are being very well looked after.'

Helena was about to make a sarcastic reply to that but she was interrupted by Antonia.

'I just can't believe you are home,' she interceded with a smile. 'Does Deborah know?'

For a moment Helena's heart missed a beat at this mention of the girl who had once been her closest friend. There had been a time shortly after Helena had left Barbados when she hadn't been able to think about Debby without feeling tearful.

'Probably.' With difficulty Helena kept her voice steady. 'You know how news travels out here. Everyone knows everything almost before it happens.'

'Well, I saw her only last week, and she didn't mention you,' Antonia continued blithely. 'She's still seeing David Cass, you know. There were rumours a while ago that they might get married.'

'Really?' Helena tried to put a brisk indifference into her voice, but it was very hard when she could feel a cold hand stealing around her heart, squeezing it unmercifully hard.

She couldn't believe that Debby would consider marrying Cass—the thought was repellent to her. For a second her composure slipped, and there was a fleeting look of anguish on her gentle features.

She glanced back at Tate. He was watching her with a look of deep contemplation in his blue eyes. Had he noticed her consternation? The notion that he had made her tilt her head up in a defiant gesture. She was damned if she was going to let anyone see how hurt she was over Debby Johnstone and Cass. That particular nightmare was over, she told herself forcefully.

'Well, I hate to interrupt this girls' reunion,' Tate drawled laconically, 'but might I suggest that we go inside? I have a few business matters I want to discuss with your father, Helena, before I leave.'

For a second Helena was so relieved that the subject had been turned away from Cass that she didn't even care why Tate was here. It was only as she turned to lead the way into the house that her priorities reasserted themselves. What manner of business was Tate here to discuss anyway? Her mouth set in a grim line as reluctantly she knocked on her father's study door.

'Ah, Tate!' Her father stood up immediately the other man entered, his face wreathed in smiles. 'Nice to see you—and you, Antonia.'

Helena stepped in and closed the door behind her firmly. Invited or not, she intended to stay and hear exactly what was going on.

'I didn't think I would need you today, Antonia, but...' Lawrence swept a hand ruefully towards the other desk at the far side of the room, which had an in-tray stacked high with correspondence. 'As you can see, it was a forlorn hope.'

'Don't worry, Mr Beaumont. I'll make short work of it,' Antonia assured him as she stepped across to take her seat.

'Meanwhile—' Tate tapped the folder that he was carrying '—I'd like to discuss those business proposals we spoke of last week.'

'Wonderful.' Lawrence sat back down behind his own desk and waved Tate towards the chair opposite. 'Helena, be a dear and get us all some coffee, will you?' he said, glancing briefly at his daughter. 'Mary has gone into Bridgetown for some shopping.'

Helena's face fell. She wanted to hear the nature of the business Tate had come to discuss, not make coffee.

Tate looked across at her, and his mouth slanted in a lop-sided grin as he took in the angry gleam in her eyes. 'Black with no sugar, thanks, Helena.'

Helena would have liked to tell him to get his own damned coffee, but courtesy and respect for her father forbade such a thing. With a dry nod, she turned to leave. She really had no other alternative.

Never had a pot of coffee been made so quickly. Helena fairly ran around the large kitchen, throwing everything on a tray. She returned to the study a few minutes later and entered the room without knocking on the door.

She was just in time to hear Tate requesting her father's signature on some document that he had placed before him. Horror welled up inside Helena as she watched her father calmly pick up his pen to comply without question.

Helena put the tray down on the desk with rather more force than she had intended, and the china cups and saucers rattled noisily in the silence. She had to say something—she couldn't just watch while her father signed a document that might be another dreadful mistake.

'Shouldn't you have professional advice before you sign anything, Pop?' she said, quietly but firmly.

Lawrence looked up, his pen poised over the paper, an expression of annoyance clear on his lined face. 'I think I'm capable of making my own decisions, Helena,' he said swiftly.

It was galling to be spoken to so curtly. She had, after all, been specially trained to advise businesses in difficulty.

'I rather thought I could be of help to you in here,' she said with gentle emphasis.

'I've told you, Helena, I've got all the help I need.' Lawrence smiled at her, totally ignoring the pleading look in his daughter's eyes. 'You go off and enjoy yourself.'

Conscious of Tate watching her, she forced herself to smile. 'Very well,' she acceded reluctantly. 'I'll see you later.'

She was quite literally fuming when she walked out of the room. How could her father be so blind as to trust Tate Ainsley with such implicit faith? And what were the documents that he was signing? All sorts of dreadful possibilities flew through her mind. Her father could be signing away Beaumont House, for all she knew.

She wandered through to the kitchen to tidy the mess she had made whilst making the coffee. It was probably best to keep busy, she thought as she wiped over the counters and put things away. Best not to think about what mistakes her father might be making.

For a brief moment she considered having a quiet word with Antonia. Perhaps she would shed some light on what was transpiring? As soon as the thought crossed her mind she dismissed it. Antonia worked for

Tate, and if past history was anything to go by the woman adored him. There was no way she would get anything out of that woman…except maybe some gossip about Debby and Cass.

Helena stopped what she was doing and leaned against the kitchen counter. Was it true that Deborah was thinking of marrying David Cass? The question returned with sudden force to haunt her.

Debby had once been like a sister to Helena. For a moment thoughts of their friendship filled her mind. They had supported each other through the ups and downs of growing up, had always been firm friends…until Cass.

'May the best girl win,' Deborah had once said laughingly, when they had both admitted to being wildly attracted to him. And then, when Cass had asked Helena out, she had shrugged and said laughingly, 'Well, luck was on your side this time.'

The words echoed hollowly inside Helena, evoking memories that she wanted so much to forget. She had dated Cass for five months. Five months of being wined and dined, and still she hadn't known the real man beneath the urbane smile.

'Helena?' Tate's velvet deep voice cut into the painful intensity of her thoughts, bringing her abruptly back to the present with a start. She turned sharply, and as she did so her arm caught the sugar bowl on the countertop, making it fall with a resounding smash onto the stone floor.

'Bit like the price of sugar,' Tate noted wryly as he came across to help her tidy up the mess. 'Plummeting all the time.'

Helena's hands trembled as she tried to pull herself sharply together. It was horrifying that just the thought

of Cass could do this to her. Her nerves were stretched,
her heart pounding. She just prayed that Tate wouldn't
notice how agitated she was.

She frowned across at him. What was he doing in
here anyway? she wondered. Presumably he had finished his shadowy business dealings with her father for
one morning… Perhaps he now thought that he could
try and sweet-talk her before he left, try and dampen
down any suspicions she might have about him?

She bit down on the softness of her lips. Well, the
man was in for a rude awakening if he thought he could
twist her around his little finger, she told herself heatedly. She knew his type, and she was well able to stand
up to him.

'I can manage to pick up the pieces, thank you,' she
told him tightly as he crouched down beside her. 'It's
something I'm quite good at—which is probably just
as well, seeing as I will be doing a lot of it around here
once the dust has settled.' Her voice was sarcastically
dry as she got in the dig that she would probably have
to pick her father's finances off the floor once Tate had
finished with him.

'I gather your father hasn't been too accommodating
about opening his accounts for you,' Tate said nonchalantly.

She glared up at him. He had come to gloat, she
thought furiously. 'Whatever gives you that idea?' She
ground the words out furiously. She certainly wasn't
about to admit any such thing to him.

'It seemed pretty obvious.' He smiled. 'Don't take
it too personally, Helena. Your father means well—it's
just an old-fashioned quirk of his that he feels
women—'

'I don't need you to tell me about my own father,'

she cut across him, her voice rising with her increasing fury. Lord, this was the final humiliation. The man was robbing them blind, and he knew damn well that she was virtually powerless to do anything because her father was too damned stubborn to let her help. He was laughing at them…it was infuriating, it was maddening.

She had to grit her teeth to keep from saying something that she might deeply regret. 'There are a lot of things you don't realise about me, Tate Ainsley,' she told him tightly. 'And one of them is that I can handle my father.'

'I'm sure you can.' Tate's voice was suddenly serious. 'But just a word of caution, Helena. Lawrence is not a well man. His blood pressure is very high, and the doctors have told him to avoid stress—'

'Thank you for your concern, Tate.' He obviously thought he could scare her into backing away from the situation. Well, he could think again. Her eyes met his with determination. 'I'm not going to upset my father…I'm going to help him.'

'As long as you understand the situation,' Tate said smoothly.

Oh, she understood, all right. She understood that Tate Ainsley was a scheming, dishonest rat.

Her hands trembled violently now, rage mixing with anxiety as she gathered up the broken crockery with swift disregard for the sharpness of the pieces.

The next moment she had cut her wrist on a jagged bit of crockery as she leaned across it. Bright red blood spilled onto the sugar, and she groaned in annoyance at such a stupid accident.

'Obviously you're not as good at picking up the pieces as you thought,' Tate grated sardonically.

She glared at him, her eyes bright with dislike.

'Here.' Before she could pull away or say anything he grabbed hold of her hand and led her over to the sink, to plunge her wrist under some running water.

The sensation of the cool water running over the cut was soothing, but Tate's hold on her arm was anything but reassuring. His closeness was totally unnerving.

'I'm fine now, thank you,' she said briskly, annoyed with herself for being so clumsy and so stupid. 'You can let go of me.'

'I think you need a plaster.' Tate completely ignored her words. 'Does Mary keep a first-aid kit in here?'

'There used to be a box in the far cupboard,' she said with a shrug.

He released her and went to investigate. 'Looks like some things don't change,' he said as he came back with some plasters and antiseptic. 'Mary always was the organised type. I could do with her at the castle.'

'I suppose you could. You seem to be intent on taking just about everything else here.' The bitter accusation spilled out before she could even think about it.

One dark eyebrow lifted at that statement, but he didn't look ruffled by it. 'Perhaps you're right,' he said calmly. 'I have Lawrence's horses, some of his land...' He let his voice trail off, and his eyes slid over Helena with cool contemplation, from her long bare legs to the malachite colour of her eyes. 'But forget Mary,' he drawled huskily, 'I think I'd prefer someone with longer legs...someone who looks good in a tennis skirt.'

The sheer audacity of that statement took her breath away. Her cheeks flared with furious colour. The man had nerve, she had to grant him that. Not only was he admitting to taking the Beaumont estate to pieces, bit by broken bit, but he was making a joke of it by luridly intimating that he would like to take her as well…

'I like seeing you speechless.' Tate grinned as he caught hold of her arm and took it out from under the water. 'I shouldn't enjoy it quite as much as I do, but I have to say there's just something about the way your skin flushes up, and your sexy lips pout, and your eyes glimmer such a beautiful shade of dark green that makes it incredible fun to wind you up.' As he was speaking he placed some cotton wool soaked with antiseptic firmly over the wound on her wrist.

She gasped, but it was more from the effrontery of his words than the stinging antiseptic.

'You have a barefaced nerve, Tate Ainsley,' she muttered between clenched teeth as he put even more antiseptic on her arm, so that it throbbed violently. 'And let me tell you that I wouldn't be interested in you if you were the only man left in Barbados.'

'Why's that?' he asked with lazy indifference. 'Don't I come up to Cass's high standards?'

She ignored that remark, and the unpleasant feeling it stirred up. 'Because you are a conceited, arrogant type and—'

'I think your father feels I might be good for you.' He cut across her, unperturbed.

'Yes, well…in my opinion my father doesn't seem to be thinking very clearly when it comes to you.'

He slanted a wry glance down at her. 'Interesting comment. Care to enlarge on it?'

'Well, for one I didn't like the way Pop just signed that document of yours without so much as reading over it,' she said quickly. 'That's just a recipe for disaster.'

'Your father knew what was in that document,' Tate

said simply as he took out a plaster and stuck it very firmly over her skin.

'Even so, he could have read it again,' she said firmly.

'Perhaps Lawrence just trusts me?' Tate lifted one eyebrow enquiringly. 'Which seems to be more than can be said of his daughter.'

She carefully avoided answering that. She would have to be very sure of her facts before she could accuse him outright. Instead she went on briskly, 'It's nothing personal, Tate, but as a financial adviser I have seen people come to grief by signing things they either don't read or don't understand.'

'Well, Lawrence is neither illiterate or stupid,' Tate said drily.

Was he justifying himself? Helena wondered in that instant. Was he saying that if Lawrence lost out in these deals it was just his own fault?

'Neither were the people I'm referring to,' she told him crossly. 'Just trusting.'

'Well, you have no need to worry about Lawrence.' Tate's voice was dismissive and offhand. 'He's my sister's husband—I'm hardly going to rip him off.'

'I'm afraid avarice is no respecter of family ties…especially the delicate ties of marriage.'

For a moment he stared at her, a strange expression on the lean, handsome features, and she had the uncomfortable feeling that she had just gone too far. 'If you're trying to insinuate—'

'I'm not trying to insinuate anything,' she cut across him hastily, a trickle of apprehension curling down her spine at the note of warning in his voice. Tate was not the type of person you threw wild accusations at—she realised that very clearly. She was going to have to tread very warily with him. 'I'm just concerned that my father has relaxed his high standards in his business dealings. Paul says he has made a lot of mistakes lately.'

'I'm afraid Paul is a bit of a lame dog where helping your father is concerned,' Tate said, his manner scathing.

'I beg your pardon?' She spluttered the words indignantly. How dared he speak about her brother in those terms?

'You heard.' Tate wasn't even slightly bothered by the look of burning resentment on her face. 'How's the wrist now?' he continued casually. 'Does it feel better?'

'No, I do not feel better.' She deliberately misunderstood him. 'In fact, I feel downright distressed that you could talk like that about my brother.'

'It's easy, believe me.' He pulled out a kitchen chair for her with a rapid movement that made her jump. 'And if you're feeling so overcome with distress perhaps you had better sit down while I clear away this mess of yours.' He turned his attention to the rest of the broken china on the floor. 'I daren't leave you to it—you might amputate your arm.'

'Ha ha!' She rasped the words abrasively.

She made no attempt to sit down, but stood watching him with a feeling of helplessness. Something about Tate was totally unnerving; he made her feel at a loss as to what to do with herself, never mind what to say to him.

He worked efficiently, clearing up the sugar and carefully wrapping the broken pieces of crockery before depositing them in the bin.

Her eyes darted to the table, where he had placed

the orange-coloured file that he had brought with him. Presumably her father had signed whatever it was he had wanted him to sign. So why hadn't Tate left for his next meeting instead of wasting his time in here? Her lips twisted in annoyance. There was an ulterior motive, of course. A man like Tate Ainsley didn't do anything unless there was something in it for him.

'Have you finished your business with my father?' she asked him crisply.

'Until tomorrow.' He turned and caught the look of annoyance and anxiety in the bright gleam of her green eyes and he sighed.

'Look, what I said about Paul...' His lips twisted drolly. 'It's nothing personal. In fact, I quite like Paul. It's just that I think he needs pulling firmly into line as far as your father and his business are concerned.'

'And I think that is none of your damned business,' she said, with a tense angry note in her voice. She knew Paul and her father had argued over Tate, and she strongly suspected that Tate had inflamed the situation, turned Lawrence's mind in his favour.

'Probably not.' He shrugged, totally insouciant. 'But I only give advice when asked.'

'Meaning that Pop asked your advice about Paul?'

'Yes, he did, as a matter of fact.'

She was incredulous. This was getting absurd. Her own father asking someone like Tate Ainsley for advice on how he should deal with his son!

'Look, Helena.' He came to stand next to her. 'I realise you are concerned about your father, about Paul. But everything will sort itself out, I'm sure of it.'

'Well, that's very reassuring.' Her voice was filled with sarcasm. 'You appear to be an absolute authority on my family—in fact, you seem to know more about them than I do.'

'Well, that's hardly surprising,' he answered coolly. 'You did take yourself off for five years.'

She flinched as if he had struck her, her eyes widening with hurt. He made it sound as if she had abandoned them. It had torn her apart to leave her home, her family. Every day in London she had thought about them, missed them. But she had been too afraid to return...it had taken a crisis to get her back.

'I didn't want to leave Barbados.' She spoke the words impulsively, without thinking. 'It certainly wasn't the easy option.'

'So why did you go?'

She met the deep blue of his eyes and came back to earth with a sharp jolt.

'A broken heart?' He ventured the words gently.

'No!' Her answer was sharp, perhaps too sharp. 'Look—' she made a deliberate attempt to calm her voice to a moderate tone '—I don't want to discuss personal issues with you. What I would like to ask is what kind of business are you conducting with my father?' She angled her chin up firmly as she held his gaze.

'I hate to remind you, Helena, but your father appears to think that his business doesn't concern you.'

It took every grain of strength to contain her rage at those words. 'Well, I think anything that concerns my father concerns me.'

'Obviously that is a point you will have to take up with Lawrence.' Tate shrugged. 'It would hardly be ethical for me to discuss his business behind his back.'

'Cut the dramatics, Tate.' She ground the words unevenly. 'You're talking to his daughter, not a rival business person.'

'Ah…but, as you so succinctly pointed out, avarice is no respecter of family ties.'

Having her own words quoted back to her was the final insult. Helena could feel her skin turning from pale ivory to vivid scarlet as she reached boiling point.

'Your sister may have married into my family, Tate Ainsley, but as far as I'm concerned you are still an outsider,' she told him with brittle fury. 'And I care about my father too deeply to let all his affairs rest in the hands of a relative stranger.'

One dark eyebrow lifted slightly. 'You mean you want to get to know me better?' he drawled laconically. 'If you hadn't just told me that I was the last man on Barbados that you would be interested in, I'd think you were fishing for a date.'

The laughing gleam in his eye filled her with a desire to hit him hard across that handsome, infuriating face.

'That's all right with me.' He shrugged. 'We'll just forget all that you've said and start again, shall we?'

'I don't know what the hell you are advocating, but I certainly don't want to go out with you on a date,' she told him in no uncertain terms, her green eyes flashing fire at him. 'I want to talk to you about—'

'Fine…dinner tonight, then.' Tate glanced at his watch. 'I've got to dash, Helena, I've got an important meeting.'

'I haven't finished,' Helena grated furiously as she watched him stroll over and collect the file from the table.

'It will have to wait until this evening, I'm afraid.' He sounded anything but afraid; he sounded totally, arrogantly sure of himself.

At that moment the kitchen door opened behind them, and much to Helena's annoyance her father came in.

'Ah, Tate, I'm glad you haven't gone,' he said cheerfully, his bright eyes moving from Helena's flushed features towards the other man's face. 'There was one last point I forgot to clear with you.'

'OK, Lawrence,' Tate drawled easily. 'I was just arranging what time I should pick your daughter up for dinner tonight.'

'Dinner, eh?' Lawrence's face lit up. 'Well, that is good news.'

Helena cringed, her skin burning with a rage that was almost feverish.

'Eight o'clock, Helena?' Tate watched her, his expression challenging and amused.

She didn't answer. It was just unbelievable that she could have allowed Tate to manoeuvre her into such a corner.

'Of course, if you don't want to talk then we'll leave it,' he said evenly.

It occurred to Helena that Tate was probably delighted to have this chance of asking her out whilst her father was here. He knew it would please Lawrence, and keeping in with Lawrence seemed of paramount importance to him.

Silence stretched for a moment, and that gleam was still in Tate's eyes. He was most likely hoping that she was going to refuse. That way he would still look good in her father's eyes for asking, plus he wouldn't have to answer any awkward questions she might put to him.

As he started to turn away, back to her father…back to more unscrupulous dealings…Helena's heart pumped unmercifully hard. She certainly didn't want to have dinner with him, but now wasn't the time to let personal feelings get in the way of finding out what was going on here.

'I suppose eight o'clock will be all right.' She made no attempt to conceal her lack of enthusiasm.

Tate turned back, a brief glimmer of triumph in his dark blue eyes.

Was he laughing at her? Helena wondered grimly.

'Wonderful,' Lawrence said loudly, as if his enthusiasm would make up for his daughter's coolness.

He was waging a losing battle. As far as Helena was concerned a dinner date with Tate was tantamount to dining with the devil himself.

CHAPTER THREE

WHAT kind of restaurant would Tate take her to? Helena wondered as she searched through her wardrobe later that day. Should she get dressed up, or should she play it low-key and casual? She didn't want to look as if she was trying to impress Tate…then again she didn't want to look underdressed.

In the end she decided on a wrap-around skirt that was long and straight, its colours a muted mixture of butter-yellow and turquoise, teamed with a soft yellow top that was strappy and cool.

Her father gave a low whistle of appreciation when she went downstairs into the lounge. 'Tate is a very lucky man,' he said with a smile.

'I'm not going out on a date,' Helena said sternly. 'It's just dinner.'

'Well, a romance has to start somewhere.' Lawrence laughed at the outraged expression on Helena's face. 'OK, OK, I won't say another word about dates or romance. I'll just say that Tate is a very charming man.'

'A very charming man.' The words rang ominously in Helena's mind. 'You've already sung Tate Ainsley's praises quite enough,' she snapped, her tone more frosty than she had intended.

Her father merely smiled, obviously thinking that she had first-date jitters. She swallowed hard. She was nervous, but not for the reasons her father thought. Her reasons for apprehension ran deeper than anyone would have guessed.

It was a long time since she had gone out on a date… Not that this was a date, she reminded herself sharply. Even so, she felt that she was putting herself in a vulnerable position by going out with Tate. She would have preferred any discussion with him to have taken place in broad daylight and in less intimate surroundings, especially as what she had to say wasn't exactly friendly.

She glanced with dread at the clock on the mantelpiece; it was nearly eight o'clock. A strange feeling of *déjà vu* trickled down her spine.

Then all at once she was remembering another date, the night of her eighteenth birthday. She felt suddenly cold and sick as the memories crowded sharply in on her. She had stood in this lounge waiting for Cass to come and pick her up…had glanced at the clock. Had joked with her father and Vivian about them being newly married and still on their honeymoon…

Every detail of that night when Cass had finally snapped, had changed from a smooth charmer into a person she hardly recognised, was imprinted forever on her brain.

She could even smell the parched heaviness of the air as the island had waited silently for an approaching storm. Could see the hotel restaurant where Cass had taken her for dinner. Hear the bitterness in his tone when she had refused his offer to stay overnight.

They hadn't spoken for most of the journey home. Cass's face had been stiff with anger, his lips set in a pinched line. Then suddenly his mood had changed again, and he had insisted she come back to his parents' house for a coffee. She had refused, but he'd swung the car in the direction of his home anyway.

She remembered the murmur of disquiet when she had gone into his house and found it empty, silent. She had turned down his offer of a whisky, but he had poured her one anyway. Then he had turned down the lights.

'I don't want a drink. I really just want to go home,' she'd said, a note of panic clear in her voice.

He hadn't answered her. Instead he'd lifted his hand and hurled the crystal glass with furious strength against the white wall of the lounge. It had hit and smashed into a million smithereens, showering the wall and the white carpet with ugly brown stains.

Helena's heart had lurched with shock at the violent action, her eyes flying from the wall to his face, absorbing the expression of loathing with a feeling of utter terror.

'You've been playing the coy little virgin and leading me on for five months, Helena, and I've had enough. Now I'm going to teach you a lesson you will never forget.'

The words had been spoken in a low tone, yet they couldn't have had more impact if he had screamed them in her face.

She remembered how she had tried to back away from him, but he had caught hold of her and flung her backwards down onto the settee with a savage strength.

The terror, the horror of it all was firmly imprinted in her mind. Just when she had thought that her lungs would burst from screaming, and that she wouldn't have enough strength to go on fighting him, the door of the lounge had burst open and Cass's mother had walked in.

For a moment the woman hadn't been sure what was going on in the room, then, as she'd turned the lights up again, there had been a horrified silence.

Helena's memories were hazy after that. She remembered that Cass had tried to say they had been making love. It had been more than obvious that he was lying.

She remembered his mother driving her home and begging her to forgive her son...

The doorbell rang, and Helena's heart lurched with a kind of crazy fear.

'The doorbell, Helena?' Her father's voice cut into the wild, chaotic thoughts.

She reached hurriedly for her bag, her hands trembling with nerves. 'I won't be late,' she murmured breathlessly, turning for the door.

'Ah...' The word trailed knowingly into the air as her father gave an exaggerated nod. 'Have a lovely evening.'

This wasn't a good idea, Helena told herself as she took a deep, steadying breath before stepping out of the front door into the warm night air.

Tate's appearance took her aback instantly. He looked incredibly handsome in a dark suit and white shirt, his hair gleaming coal-black, in the moonlight.

He smiled, his teeth very white against his tanned skin, his eyes raking over her appearance, noting every detail. The gleam of male appreciation in his blue eyes did nothing to lessen Helena's nerves—in fact, her apprehension increased in one wild terrific surge.

'Good evening, Helena. May I say you look very beautiful tonight?'

'Tate is a very charming man.' The words ran through her mind. And the shadow of David Cass seemed to bear down on her again, so that she could almost imagine his voice…his face in front of her for a moment.

'Helena?'

Aware suddenly that Tate was looking at her strangely now, she gathered herself together and smiled at him. Her smile, for all her efforts, was rather wan, her skin pale.

'Are you all right?'

'Of course.' Her voice held just the faintest hint of a tremor.

He held out his hand to help her down the steps towards the car, but she pointedly ignored the chivalrous gesture, preferring not to make any contact with him, however small.

If Tate noticed anything amiss in her manner he made no comment. He followed her down the steps and then opened the passenger door for her. Helena settled herself into the comfortable leather seat, telling herself firmly that the nervous reaction she had felt a moment ago was really stupid.

History wouldn't repeat itself; all men were not like David Cass. It was a phrase she had used many times over the years to still the beating of her heart when a man put his hand on her, or looked at her with too much intensity. Usually it helped in some small measure to calm the rapid beat of her heart, but tonight the apprehension, the nerves didn't even begin to die away.

The car sped down the drive, the powerful lights cutting the velvet darkness of the night.

'So where are we going?' From somewhere Helena summoned up a light, casual tone.

'I thought I'd take you to my place,' he said smoothly.

Helena's heart missed a beat. Was he talking about

the hotel he owned at Ainsley Point? She prayed sincerely that he was. 'The Ainsley Hotel?' she asked
lightly.

'No, I thought that my home would be more private.
I've arranged for one of my top chefs to cook for us.'
He flicked a searching glance at her. 'So we will be
alone to talk.'

Cold fear clutched at Helena, squeezing her unmercifully in its cruel grip. She didn't want to be alone
with Tate.

The memory of that date long ago with Cass reared
its ugly head for another few dizzying seconds.

Desperately she swallowed down the queasy sensations uncurling slowly in the pit of her stomach. That
wasn't going to happen, she rationalised swiftly. This
was a business dinner, not a date. All the same, they
would be alone...she would be in a vulnerable position.

'I'd rather have gone to the hotel,' she said stiffly.

'Why?' He shot her a puzzled look.

'Well...' She shrugged and looked away from him,
uncomfortable under his probing stare. She could
hardly say that she was afraid to be alone with him—
it wouldn't be sensible to admit her fear of him. She
had to appear confident, coolly aloof. 'Because this
isn't a date. I thought I made myself clear this morning
that I want some answers on your business dealings
with my father.'

'Really?' There was wry amusement in his tone now.
'I thought we were going to forget all that? You know,
it's not so long ago that you told me you wouldn't
discuss business with me. I'm that fox, remember, the
one intent on getting into the winter store you've
stocked up...'

Crazy as it was, that quite ludicrous statement made

her relax slightly, and she gave a laugh—half in relief at the lessening of tension inside her, half at the utter absurdity of those words.

'So what exactly is it that you are all fired up about?' Tate continued, with a mocking lift of one eyebrow.

She forced herself to turn slightly in her seat and look at him directly. 'To be specific, my father's investments,' she said crisply.

'I see.' The words trailed heavily into the darkness. 'With the greatest respect, I think we covered that issue this morning, and I told you that you should be discussing your father's business with your father. Haven't you asked him?'

She had tried to engage her father in a conversation about business this afternoon, but he had been maddeningly evasive. She didn't want to tell Tate Ainsley that, however, he would find it very gratifying, very amusing. 'Well, yes...' she started hesitantly.

'Good, then you don't need to ask me, do you?' he concluded briskly.

'Well, I do, actually,' she insisted. 'I've rather gained the impression over the last twenty-four hours that you seem to know more about my father's business than my father.' She was proud of the way she kept her voice cool, unemotional. She had to find out what was going on without making direct accusations... She had to keep her temper if she was to play a balancing act between her father and Tate.

'Well, I don't know where you got that impression, but it's not true.' His tone was just as cool as hers.

'Paul mentioned—'

'Ah, we're back to Paul.' Tate cut across her, his voice rasping with indifference and with sardonic humour. 'Sorry, Helena, but I've already given you my opinion of your brother's business sense. I'm not going through that minefield again.'

Helena bristled at the condescending tone, her loyalty to her brother rising indignantly. She had gone to see Paul at his apartment in Bridgetown today and their reunion had been overshadowed by his depression over Lawrence's cool treatment of him and his anger towards Tate. He had certainly not been amused when she had told him she was having dinner with Tate.

'That will achieve nothing, Helena,' he had said furiously. 'Except perhaps that the man will set you against me as he has set my father against me.'

'I wouldn't underestimate my brother if I were you, Tate,' she said, a warning note in her voice. Anger glinted in her eyes. If he thought he could poison her mind against her own brother he could think again.

'I'll give you ten out of ten for the protective sister act,' he drawled with some amusement.

'Whereas you don't give a damn about anybody or anything except making money, do you, Tate?' she said heatedly.

He shrugged, not one bit put out by the accusation. 'I wouldn't go so far as to say that. But, yes, business has been a priority over these last few years.'

The man had gall, she had to give him that. He was ruthless and determined, and he didn't give a damn who knew it.

'Is it true that you have advised my father to take unnecessary risks in business?' she asked him now, in a clearly derisive tone.

Tate laughed. It was a cool laugh, unlike his usual warm tones. 'Someone once said that to get profit without risk, experience without danger, reward without work is as impossible as it is to live without being born.'

Helena glared at him. It seemed that getting any kind of straight answer from Tate Ainsley was not going to be easy. But then what had she expected? she asked herself grimly. Tate wasn't a straightforward person.

An uneasy silence hung between them while Helena sought to find the right words to put this infuriating man in his place. The words remained elusive as the tall and imposing gates to the castle loomed ahead.

The driveway to Tate's home was straight, lined with tall palm trees. In the old days the tall palms had been used by plantation owners as weather barometers—one glance out at them and they had been able to see clearly which way the wind was blowing. In the Ainsley estate's case Tate's ancestor Black Jack had taken special note of the weather for a much more sinister purpose.

The legend of Black Jack Ainsley still lived on in Barbados to this very day. Some said that he had been a ruthless man—a man who had lived under a cloak of respectability in the castle on the cliffs. By day he had been the charming landowner, rich and powerful, but at night, when the weather had been right, he had hung lanterns along the rocks at Ainsley Point, mercilessly luring ships into their watery graves to plunder their cargo.

At that time the Ainsley estate had been devoted to sugar cane, just as Beaumont House had been. But since then, as Tate had pointed out, the decline in the value of sugar had meant each estate had had to look towards other resources to make money. In Tate's case he had built a massive hotel in his grounds.

Helena had never been into the Ainsley Hotel, but it was supposed to be one of the most luxurious on the island. It also boasted an exclusive health club and its own private beach.

They passed the turning that was signposted to the hotel and kept straight on. Soon she was able to see the impressive outline of the castle turrets against the silver darkness of the sky.

When they rounded a corner and drew up in front of the castle she was momentarily taken aback.

The last time she had seen this place it had been in a dreadful state of disrepair. Now it stood magnificently floodlit, tall and slightly austere, but beautifully restored.

'Home sweet home.' Tate looked across at her. 'Shall we shelve all this talk about family and business until later? I, for one, just want to relax for a while and enjoy a pleasant meal in the company of a beautiful woman.'

'Why, is someone else coming?' she asked, her voice scathing. She was uncomfortable with compliments like that. She was not easily flattered and she didn't like smooth-talkers—especially those that she might be left alone with.

On the rare occasions when Helena went out on a date she was always very careful to choose crowded restaurants and public places. Being alone with a man made her feel vulnerable…it made her remember things she would much rather forget.

'You know I was referring to you,' he said gently.

'Well, don't. I don't find your personal remarks flattering and I'm not here to be sweet-talked.' Her answer was abrupt, and she made no effort to soften it.

To her discomfort he didn't look in the slightest bit chastened. His lips twisted in that attractive smile of his. 'You are a real spoilsport, do you know that?'

Her heart bounded fiercely against her ribcage and back again. 'I'm not playing games, Tate,' she assured him stiffly. 'I'm not interested in a romantic interlude. I want to make that quite clear before I come inside with you.'

'Oh, you've made yourself clear enough.' He didn't sound annoyed, just wryly amused as he reached for the doorhandle and stepped out, leaving her no option but to follow.

She breathed the salty tang of the night air, trying to still her nervous thoughts. It was ridiculous to feel so afraid about being alone with Tate, she told herself crossly. Ainsley Castle was probably filled to capacity with staff; they wouldn't be alone—not in the real sense of the word. Nevertheless, despite the warm temperature, she shivered.

Tate came around to join her. 'Cold?' he asked softly.

She shook her head, his observant question only serving to worry her further. The man didn't miss anything, not a flicker of her eyelashes or a shiver down her spine.

Her eyes flicked over him. The light from the castle highlighted his dark, rugged good looks—it also caught the jagged scar that ran down one side of his cheek, making it look vivid-white against the tanned perfection of his skin. For one crazy second in that strange half-light he looked almost medieval. The image was so sharp that she caught her breath. He looked just as she imagined Black Jack would have.

She swallowed hard and chastised herself. She was being foolish.

The castle door swung smoothly open, and Tate stood back for her to enter.

CHAPTER FOUR

IT FELT cooler inside, probably due as much to the thickness of the walls as the air-conditioning. The hallway was large, with a sweeping staircase that branched halfway up leading to different sides of the residence. Dominating everything at the turn of the stairs was an enormous stained glass window that would probably look tremendous during the day.

Tate opened one of the doors to the left and led her into an exceptionally beautiful room. It was heavily beamed with dark mahogany and a long banqueting table was laid with silver candelabra whose flickering flames reflected in the deeply polished wood. Two solitary places were laid at the top. The subdued lighting gave an atmosphere of intimacy, also an air of stepping back in time.

'Can I interest you in a pre-dinner drink?' Tate crossed to the far side of the room, where comfortable armchairs sat either side of a crackling log fire.

'Just an orange juice, please.' She wasn't about to start drinking alcohol; she wanted to keep her wits very firmly about her. She followed him and sat gracefully in one of the chairs by the fire. 'It's unusual to see a fire like that in Barbados,' she said idly as she stared into the flickering flames. 'There's a flower arrangement in our fireplace at home.'

He laughed. 'I suppose that's a hangover from my

mother's day. She always asked my father to light the fires. She missed her home in England terribly. Longed for the cold winters and roaring log fires.'

Helena relaxed a little and laughed. 'I bet once she went back to England she missed the sunshine.'

'Yes.' He handed her a long-stemmed crystal glass. 'Strangely enough, she also missed my father.' He returned to the drinks cabinet and poured himself a whisky.

Helena knew that Tate's parents had separated when he was young. She didn't know the exact details, but she knew that his father had been a womaniser.

Apparently, when Tate's mother had discovered that her husband was having numerous affairs, she had taken Tate and Vivian back to live with her in her native England. Once she had left, Saul Ainsley had let his estate go rapidly downhill. The castle had fallen into a terrible state of disrepair.

Helena watched as Tate took the seat opposite her. 'Do you think your father missed his family?'

Tate shrugged. 'I didn't see much of Saul. He wasn't one for fatherly duties.'

Helena knew that Tate had not visited his father very often. He had left for England when he wasn't very old and had only come back to live in Barbados a year after Saul had died. That was about eight years ago now.

'What about your mother—is she still alive?' Helena asked curiously.

'Yes, she lives in Cornwall. She visits sometimes, but she is never happy here. I suppose this place brings back too many memories for her.'

The door at the far end of the room opened and a

young woman came in. 'Would you like me to serve dinner now, sir?'

'Yes, thank you, Joy.' Tate stood up and led the way to the table. Politely he pulled out a chair, and held it while Helena sat down.

'You didn't need to go to so much trouble for me, Tate,' Helena said as a delicious starter of avocado and prawns was put down in front of them.

'It's no trouble, believe me,' Tate said. 'Besides, it's worth it just to please Lawrence. He looked thrilled when he heard that I was picking you up for dinner.'

'And you like to keep in my father's good books, don't you, Tate?' she said archly.

Tate shrugged. 'I like Lawrence a lot—I have great respect for him.'

These words totally threw Helena. How could you respect someone and swindle them at the same time? The answer was easy—you couldn't. Tate was either lying through his teeth or he honestly believed that he was not to blame for her father's financial downfall. A lot of confidence tricksters were likeable rogues, she reminded herself sharply. A lot of them lied to themselves, never mind their victims.

'That's why you send over your secretary to help him, presumably?' she asked crisply. 'And that's why you have advised him so…expertly on his business affairs?' Her voice was heavily tinged with sarcasm.

'I do my best.' Tate's voice was relaxed with no hint of any angry undertones. 'For Vivian as much as your father.'

Helena stared at him. Did he even care about Vivian? The man was hard-headed and shrewd, for all his laid-back *bonhomie*.

'You seem to have been tremendously successful in

a very short space of time,' she observed cynically. 'When I left Barbados your hotel was just being built. I believe it is now a very thriving concern.'

'I can't complain. Come and have a look around one day,' he said easily. 'And, of course, if you would like to go horse riding any time just phone through and I'll arrange for a horse to be made available for you— preferably your old one, Gypsy. I believe you used to be very fond of that animal.'

Helena's chest tightened painfully. Her horse had been very dear to her. Her being owned by this pirate of a man broke her heart.

'Yes, I was.' Her voice was grim. She was damned if she was going to thank Tate for the offer of her own horse. 'Tell me, why did you buy all my father's horses?'

'A lot of my hotel guests like to go riding.' Tate finished his food and leaned back in his chair to regard her laconically from bright blue eyes.

That wasn't the answer she'd wanted. She had wanted to know why her father had sold the horses in the first place, but of course she had phrased the question wrongly. She would have to weigh her words more carefully in the future, she thought, annoyed with herself over the slip.

'So poor old Gypsy has been relegated to the ranks of hacking, being ridden by strangers who probably don't even know how to ride.'

'At least she's being ridden,' Tate said drily. 'I can assure you she is well looked after. The grooms go to a lot of trouble to make sure they select the right mount for the right person.'

Helena didn't say anything to that. She felt a bit guilty about her outburst. As Tate had said…at least

Gypsy was being ridden. 'I'm surprised my father sold the horses at all,' she said, with a shake of her head. 'He had some of the finest animals on the island. They were a great passion of his.'

'And also of yours, by the sound of it,' Tate answered lightly. 'In fact there's strong emotion in your voice and in your eyes when you talk to me about anything connected with your home here. I'm surprised, given the obvious strength of your love for the place, that you ever left.' His eyes met hers, steady and direct. 'I can only assume that the reason behind your departure was one almighty powerful one.'

Helena looked away from him, disconcerted by the directness of his gaze and the perceptive tone of that remark. 'I think I've already told you—I was offered a wonderful job. Too good to turn down.'

'Ah, yes, the bank.' His voice was dry.

Something about his derogatory tone irritated her intensely. 'You don't care much for the banking establishment, do you, Tate?' she asked with a frown.

'I have nothing against it.' He spread his hands expressively. 'Banks have never done me any harm, and then again they've never done me any favours. But in my humble opinion a bank only wants to do you favours when you don't need them.'

'That's not strictly true,' she said quickly.

'Isn't it?' There was a gleam of laughter in his eyes. 'But then you would say that, wouldn't you? Don't you ever long to break free from the rigid constraints that the bank places on you? Don't you long to use initiative and gut feeling rather than follow a straight set of rules?'

'There is nothing wrong with following rules,' she

told him stiffly. 'Guidelines are laid down for the customers' protection.'

'Ah, yes.' He nodded his head sagely, yet there was a mocking gleam in his eyes.

'You like to take risks, don't you, Tate?' she asked suddenly.

'If the risk is well thought out in advance and I've weighed up all the angles.'

Was that what he had done with her father? Weighed up the dangers of being found out, the risks of being caught out and branded a con man? 'You mean you're calculating,' she said, with an edge of derision in her voice.

He merely laughed at that. 'You know, there is an old saying in the Caribbean: "No call alligator Long Mouth till you pass him".' Humour danced in the depths of his eyes.

She shook her head, and had to laugh at the absurd comment. 'You've just made that up.'

'Indeed, I have not,' he said with a grin. 'And you should laugh more often,' he added suddenly. 'You're exceptionally beautiful when you smile—your whole face lights up—'

'Don't smooth-talk me, Tate,' she cut across him abruptly, her laughter dying. 'I don't like it.'

'I wasn't smooth-talking you.' He was unperturbed by her sharpness. 'Don't be so suspicious. I was merely making a friendly observation.'

Was she overly suspicious? She stared into his eyes. They reminded her of the Caribbean Sea on a calm, sultry, hot day. Surely somebody with eyes like this couldn't be all bad? she asked herself abstractedly. Then again, sharks lurked beneath the silky deep waters of the Caribbean.

Tate was obviously a man who took chances where he could—a man who played hard and for very high stakes. Was he also totally unscrupulous? The answer remained elusive.

Despite the evidence of Lawrence selling everything off to him, despite what Paul had told her of shady dealings, there were moments when she wanted to keep an open mind...moments when she almost hoped that Paul had got things wrong. Moments of insanity, she told herself briskly as she studied him across the table.

His face was half in shadow, and candlelight flickered over the jagged scar, highlighting the livid-white mark like a bolt of lightning against the dark tan of his skin. She remembered the gossip when Tate had come back to live in Barbados after his father's death. She remembered people saying that he looked like his ancestor Black Jack, that he too had had a scar running down the left-hand side of his face.

Black Jack's had been caused by a sword fight, they said... But then there were so many different stories about that man that probably nobody would ever know for sure which were true, they had been so distorted by time...

'Can I ask you a personal question, Tate?' she murmured in a moment of impulse.

One eyebrow lifted. 'You can ask,' he said wryly.

'Is it true that you resemble your ancestor, Black Jack?' Her eyes moved over his face again. 'I've heard it said that you're the living image of him...and that he also had a scar that ran down the side of his face.'

She asked the question just as the young waitress came into the room with their main course. It was obvious that she had heard the words from the expression on her face. She looked at Helena in a way that told her she considered her either extremely brave or extremely foolish—perhaps both.

Tate merely smiled. It was an enigmatic smile, tinged with sardonic humour. He waited until the waitress had put their meals in front of them and was heading for the door again before he made a reply. 'There's a painting of him upstairs—I'll show you later, if you like. You can judge for yourself.'

Was that some kind of ploy to get her upstairs? she wondered nervously. The door closed, leaving them alone again, and Helena's hands tightened nervously in her lap. 'Is that tantamount to asking me to come up and see your etchings?'

One eyebrow lifted, and his eyes glittered with amusement. 'When I want to make love to you, Helena, I will say so. I don't believe in subterfuge.'

Her skin flooded with colour at such an arrogant statement. 'You are very sure of yourself, Tate Ainsley.'

'And you are very cynical. Tell me, does your mistrust of men date back to Cass?'

Her eyes flew back to his, and despite all her efforts her cheeks burned even more fiercely. 'Certainly not!' But even as she denied his words a small voice was asking if perhaps he had a point. She *had* kept her distance from men since Cass. Determinedly she blocked out the thought. She didn't want to admit that Cass could influence any part of her life.

'I've already told you that I've forgotten about David Cass.' She glared at him, her eyes wide and shimmering.

'I know what you told me,' he said with a shrug. 'But I couldn't help noticing how upset you were today when Antonia mentioned that Cass and Debby might be getting married.'

'I wasn't in the slightest bit upset…a little surprised, maybe.' She maintained her cool composure with the greatest of difficulty. Tate's blue eyes seemed to burn into her with a question. 'I didn't think that Cass would be Debby's type.' She looked away from him as she spoke. Even mentioning Cass's name was painful…she didn't want to think about that man, never mind discuss his relationship with Debby.

'But you know that they have been seeing each other for years…since Cass finished with you.'

'Cass didn't finish with me.' She spoke the words without thinking, and there was far too much raw emotion in her voice, in her eyes too, and she knew instantly that she was betraying too much in those few seconds. Her hurt…her fury…was there for Tate to see, and she hated the fact that he could scratch her surface so easily and see how vulnerable she was where David Cass was concerned. She also hated Cass for what he had done to her.

'Well, whatever…it was his loss.'

Tate's gentle comment took her by surprise, and for a moment she couldn't find any words to reply—no bland comments, not even a way to switch the subject.

'So, anyway, you haven't told me what you think of the lobster?' he said nonchalantly.

'It's…it's excellent. You have a good chef.' She forced a smile to her lips, but it didn't quite hide the shadows in the deep green of her eyes.

His gaze moved over the paleness of her complexion contemplatively. 'You're very kind, considering you've hardly touched the food at all.'

The warmth of Tate's tone threw her, as did the way

he was deliberately swinging the conversation away from the murky subject of Cass. He had seen her reaction, weighed it up and then swiftly changed tack. She couldn't fathom Tate at all. One moment he was the reckless villain, the next he seemed almost human.

'Of course I have.' She toyed with an asparagus spear in an attempt to look as if she was enjoying the meal.

'Well, I'd value your honest opinion. This chef is new... He comes with top qualifications and references, but even so I want to be sure he's got what it takes before I offer him a position in my new hotel.'

'You're opening a new hotel?' He had her full attention now. 'On Barbados?'

He nodded. 'The Caribbean side of the island.'

'You certainly move fast.' Helena shook her head in amazement.

'I don't believe in letting the grass grow.'

'That's fine, as long as you don't overstretch yourself.'

He smiled at that. 'There speaks a true financial adviser.'

She shrugged. 'Starting another business is always a risk—'

'It's a calculated risk,' he interrupted with a grin, throwing up his hands ruefully.

She looked at him and had to laugh. 'I suppose I do tend to err on the side of caution,' she admitted with a shrug. 'It's just that I've seen a lot of businesses go bankrupt because they've over-extended themselves.'

'The bank sends you in as a kind of rescue line, does it?'

'Sometimes.' She smiled. 'But mostly my job necessitates that I sit in at shareholders' meetings within large companies. My task is to protect the bank's interests within the company and give good solid advice for future financial growth.'

'I bet they don't know what's hit them when you turn up in those boardrooms,' Tate said, with a wry twist of his lips.

Helena frowned. 'I'll have you know that I am very good at my job, Tate.'

'Oh, I believe you.' Tate shook his head. 'Actually, I could do with someone like you on my team. Someone with both feet steadily on the ground to throw words of caution at me when I have wild new ideas.'

Helena laughed at that. 'I've got the feeling that no matter how many words of caution I threw in you would still do exactly your own thing.'

'But I wouldn't shout at you if you said I told you so.' For a moment his eyes moved with tantalising thoroughness over the smooth contours of her face, lingering on the full, generous curve of her lips.

Immediately Helena could feel herself tensing up again, and she suddenly realised that in a short space of time Tate had succeeded in making her forget her anguish over Cass…had made her forget who she was dealing with. She had been chatting with him as if he was an old friend. What was more she had been enjoying herself!

Annoyance flared. She wasn't here to enjoy herself, she was here to find out what was going on…to find out what Tate Ainsley was up to.

'So…' Her eyes narrowed on him. 'You were telling me about your new hotel.' She brought the subject swiftly back to business. Had Tate overstretched himself financially…was this the reason he was swindling her father? 'You say it's on the Caribbean side of the island? Where, exactly?'

'That piece of land I bought from your father,' he replied nonchalantly, and leaned across to refill her wine glass. 'Bounty Bay.'

For a moment Helena's heart missed a beat. Bounty Bay was the most beautiful and the most unspoilt place she knew. The sand was sugar spun white, the trees were thick and luxuriant, and the smell of wild flowers permeated the salt air. 'You've built on Bounty Bay?' Horror was clear in her tone.

'Well, I didn't buy it to go swimming,' he drawled sardonically. 'It was a business move.'

She should have guessed when Paul had told her that her father had sold that land. She should have known that Tate would build there, but somehow it was a terrible shock. She shook her head, and dislike for the man gleamed clearly in her eyes. 'How much did you pay for that land?' she asked sharply as she remembered her brother saying that he had got it for a song.

One eyebrow lifted. 'I think that is between your father and me...is it not?' he enquired silkily.

In other words he was too embarrassed to tell her, she thought furiously. 'You know that land was my mother's originally. It was in her family for a number of years.' Her voice trembled slightly.

Bounty Bay was very dear to her heart. It was a place Helena had often gone to when she was feeling low or when something was worrying her. It had always soothed her, and somehow when she was there she had felt that her mother wasn't very far away.

'Your father did mention it.' Tate was unconcerned. 'You'll have to come out and have a look around. I think you'll be pleasantly surprised.'

'Oh, nothing you do will surprise me, Tate,' she assured him in a voice laced with bitter irony. She would have liked to say more on the subject, she would have liked to pour out all Paul's words and accusations in that moment, but with difficulty she held her tongue. The waitress came back to take their plates and ask what they would like for dessert.

'I couldn't eat another mouthful,' Helena declared emphatically. In fact she had managed to eat more than she had thought she would manage. 'The meal was delicious.'

'Just coffee, then, please, Joy.' Tate pushed his chair back from the table and moved to assist Helena. 'Would you like to see that painting of Black Jack now, Helena?' he invited smoothly.

About to refuse, she noticed the challenging look on his handsome features. He thought she was afraid of him!

Her lips set in a determined line; she wouldn't allow him to believe that. 'Why not?' She shrugged carelessly. It was a shrug that belied a tremor of nerves.

He led the way out of the room and up the steep stairs in silence. Portraits lined the walls and they were all austere and dark, somehow sinister. Helena felt as if all the eyes were following her, watching her with looks of displeasure.

'Are these all your ancestors?' She waved towards the paintings and he grinned.

'Yes. Cheerful-looking bunch, aren't they?'

'They give me the creeps,' she said honestly, then, realising she had just insulted his relatives, not to mention his property, she clamped a hand to her mouth. 'I didn't mean that to sound rude,' she said hastily.

'Oh, I'll forgive you,' he said, with a gleam of laughter in his voice. 'But I'm not so sure if they will.'

At that moment the soft light that had blazed from the overhead chandeliers went out, and they were plunged into inky black darkness.

'Tate!' Helena's voice lifted as panic threatened to swamp her.

'It's all right.' His voice was calm and deeply reassuring. 'It's only our erratic electricity supply, not the wrath of my glamorous relations.' His hand reached out and found hers. 'Watch your step, and don't worry—the generator should cut in any moment.'

She allowed him to lead her up the remaining stairs. Her heart was thumping painfully against her chest as fear encircled her. It was crazy to be afraid, but suddenly she was thinking of Cass, remembering the evening that was burnt forever on the deepest part of her soul.

They reached the top of the stairs, and as Helena's eyes grew accustomed to the dark she could just make out a table to one side of them.

'You can let go now,' Tate said gently, and she realised that she was still clinging very tightly to his hand.

'Sorry,' she muttered with embarrassment.

'Oh, I have no objection to you holding my hand,' he said with humour. 'It must be every man's dream to have a financial adviser holding his hand so tightly.'

Her teeth grated at the sardonic comment. 'I wasn't afraid,' she said sharply. 'I just didn't want to fall.'

'Of course.' His voice was annoyingly unconvinced.

'And there's no need to be facetious,' she grated angrily. 'I didn't find your wisecrack remotely amusing.'

'It was a joke, Helena.'

'Well, it wasn't a funny joke.' Her voice trembled with reaction. 'It was the kind of inane comment a boring sexist male would make.' She knew she was overreacting completely, but she couldn't seem to help herself.

There was the sound of a match being struck, and then a flickering gold light warmed the darkness as Tate lifted up an oil lamp.

His eyes moved over the pallor of her skin, the eyes that looked impossibly wide for such a small face.

'I'm sorry, Helena,' he said calmly, then reached out a hand to touch her face. She flinched back from him instinctively, and a shiver of pure terror raced down her spine. 'Don't...don't touch me.'

His eyes narrowed. 'I wasn't going to hurt you.'

'No...of course not.' Desperately she strove to get her wayward emotions under control before he thought her a complete fool.

'Are you OK?' The note of deep concern in his voice was almost her undoing.

'Of course I'm OK.' She turned away from him before he noticed the tears that shimmered in her eyes. 'So where is this painting?' she forced herself to ask briskly.

'Just a little further along.' There was a puzzled note in his voice, but to her relief he moved ahead of her to lead the way.

The oil lamp cast strange distorted shadows against the walls. Helena's breathing was uneven as she tried to pull herself together.

'There.' Tate held the lamp up and the golden light spilled over a painting that held Helena spellbound for a moment.

Black Jack stood on the cliffs. Behind him a storm

raged over the fierce Atlantic Ocean, but he seemed untouched by its ferocious strength. There was an incredible power about the figure—his shoulders were wide, his long legs set slightly apart in an almost arrogant stance.

But it was his face that held Helena. His eyes were deep blue, and as fierce as the sea behind him, and his skin was palely dramatic against the jet-black sweep of his hair.

'Sorry to disappoint you, but as you can see Black Jack had no scar.' Tate's voice distracted her, and she looked around at him.

It was like looking at a mirror image, scar or no scar. Tate Ainsley was the living image of Black Jack Ainsley.

The lights came back on at that moment, dispelling the eerie feeling that she had stepped back in time.

Tate put the oil lamp back on one of the polished tables before turning to look at her.

'Feel better now?' His voice had dropped to a gentle level, and his eyes seemed to be probing so deeply that she was afraid for a moment that they could see right into her innermost thoughts.

'Yes, of course.' She tried her very best to shrug the incident off with an airy show of humour. 'It's just so embarrassing to have to admit you're still frightened of the dark at the age of twenty-four.'

Even though Tate smiled at that she had the distinct impression that she hadn't fooled him for one minute.

CHAPTER FIVE

TATE moved a step closer towards her, his lips twisted in an arrogantly amused smile and his blue eyes sweeping over her body, a blatant look of desire in their smoky depths.

Helena felt a wave of heat rush through her, and her breath caught in deep painful spasms as he stretched out a hand to run it smoothly over the side of her face and down the tender column of her neck.

Every sense seemed tuned to his touch, and even the soft downy hair along her skin seemed to prickle with a kind of electricity at the sensation of his hand against her skin. A pulse beat rapidly at the hollow of her throat.

His eyes moved towards that violent pulse, then down to the low-cut line of her top, where her breasts moved with the fierce heaviness of her breathing.

'You are a very beautiful woman, Helena.' He drawled the words huskily; they were like honey dripping into the hot stillness around them. 'And I'd like very much to make love to you.'

She swallowed hard and tried to find her voice, but it seemed to have deserted her.

His hand moved from her throat, down over the smooth bareness of her shoulder. 'Do you hear me, Helena? I want you...I know you want me.'

He moved closer; she could feel his breath against

her heated skin. 'Tell me you want me...' His voice rasped like silk against sandpaper.

'I...' She tried to deny him... She tried desperately to speak...but her voice wouldn't function. Her heart felt like a wild caged creature inside her as his lips came closer towards hers. She moistened their dryness, heat and sudden longing sweeping through her in a wild, sweet rush. 'Yes.' She breathed the word into the tropical heat of the night; it was just a whisper, but a whisper of intense longing. 'Yes...'

Her eyes were heavy, as heavy as her body felt. She longed to feel his hands against her naked skin. She longed for him to kiss her, wildly, passionately, with sweet desire.

'Tate.' She whispered his name into the hot silence, her heart pumping madly, filling her ears, filling her body with the sharp, heavy sound of its lifebeat...

Her gaze moved over his face, over its rugged attractiveness. He had...grey eyes. Her heart stopped beating and the world seemed to stand still. It wasn't Tate who was breathing so close to her ear...it wasn't Tate's mouth that was coming down towards her...it was Cass's. She was with David Cass. Her breath caught in her throat and then released in a chilling long scream.

She could hear his laughter vibrating through the hot silence and the darkness. Her eyes opened wildly; she was staring into heavy blackness.

It took several moments for her to realise that she had been dreaming...and they were moments of complete terror.

With a trembling hand she reached to put the bedside lamp on. She felt a little better as the bright light chased the dark shadows away and she was surrounded by the cosy familiarity of her bedroom, but even so it took a while for the wild beating of her heart to return to something like normal.

For a moment her dream of Tate returned to haunt her mind, disturbing in its intensity. It had been so seductive that even now, just thinking about it, she felt hot again...hot and unbearably tense.

It was just a stupid dream, she told herself crossly. As for the nightmare about David Cass—for months after she had left Barbados her sleep had been haunted by visions of that man. Visions of him touching her, his lips hot against hers. But she had thought that she had beaten Cass, and the dreams had stopped a long time ago. Obviously being back at home with everyone mentioning his name had been what had prompted them again.

She turned restlessly, staring up at the overhead fan as it sent wafts of air against her heated skin. She had lost everything through David Cass—her peace of mind...her best friend. Since that night she hadn't been able to relax in a man's company—she was always watching, weighing every word, every movement.

For a moment she found herself remembering Tate's words to her this evening. 'Does your mistrust of men date back to Cass?' Although she was loath to admit it, he was right.

Her mind turned towards the evening she had just spent with Tate. Surprisingly, except for the incident with the lights, it hadn't been as much of an ordeal as she had expected. There had been moments when she had found herself quite enjoying Tate's company.

Her lips tightened with annoyance. Paul would have been disgusted with her if he'd known she could be so easily distracted. She had agreed to have dinner with

Tate to find out what was going on about her father's finances. She had discovered nothing...nothing except for the fact that Tate had a surprisingly warm side...a smile that could brighten the darkest sky.

When he had driven her home at the end of the evening he had been very pleasant, so charming. When they'd drawn up outside Beaumont House he had wished her goodnight politely, had thanked her for her company. She had been relieved when he'd made no move to kiss her...relieved and surprised.

Why should she even have thought he would kiss her? she asked herself heatedly now. What the hell was the matter with her anyway? Their evening hadn't been a romantic date. Tate had only asked her out because he wanted to keep on the right side of her father. She really should have learnt her lesson where charming men were concerned by now.

For a moment she remembered her dream of Tate's hands caressing her skin, his lips close to hers...her words asking him to make love to her.

Her face burned with the shame of it. Groaning, she turned and buried her head into the pillows. She had to try and get some sleep. Tomorrow she would phone Paul...and she would have to admit to him that having dinner with the enemy had achieved nothing. Perhaps he could suggest her next move, because she was fast drawing a blank.

Paul, however, was maddeningly unavailable the next day. Helena hung around the house all morning, hoping he might ring, but silence reigned supreme over Beaumont House. Helena ventured into her father's office, but her tentative offer of help was met with the usual rebuttal. Obviously this tack was not going to work.

At midday, feeling like a cat on a hot plate, she borrowed Vivian's car and decided to go for a drive. She didn't set out with the intention of going to Bounty Bay, but somehow, as if on automatic pilot, she found herself gravitating towards it.

She pulled the car into the side of the road as the sign for Bounty came into view. Her eyes scanned the narrow twisting lane that dipped down towards the coast. Except for the palm trees, and the flamboyant trees with their flame-red blossom, she might have been looking at a lush piece of the English countryside. The scene was just the same as it had always been: rolling green fields and a thick forest of trees that blanketed the ground until the sparkle of the blue Caribbean Sea. There was no sign of a hotel at all.

She heaved a sigh of relief. All sorts of terrible pictures had flashed through her mind when Tate had told her he had built here. At least he hadn't torn up all the trees.

She switched off the ignition and decided to walk down to have a closer look—that way there would be less likelihood of drawing attention to herself.

The sun was beating down with cruel intensity, with only a slight breeze to ruffle the corners of Helena's forget-me-not-blue summer dress. Then the hotel came into view and she forgot about the heat—forgot about everything except the fact that Tate Ainsley had come a hell of a long way in a short space of time. The hotel was fabulous.

'You're on private property, miss. Please state your business.'

The brisk voice cut the tranquil silence of the afternoon, and Helena turned with a start to see a uniformed guard on the path behind her.

Her heart sank. All she had wanted was a quick, unobtrusive look around; now Tate was bound to find out that she had been here.

'I'm a friend of Mr. Ainsley's,' she answered briskly as the guard came closer.

He nodded. 'Well, Mr. Ainsley is in his office, if you would like to follow me.'

She really had no option but to turn and follow the man as he led the way down to the main doors. The last person she wanted to see today was Tate Ainsley, and her nerves twisted anxiously as she tried to think of some excuse for calling here at all.

The Bounty Bay Hotel was magnificent inside; obviously no expense had been spared in its decor. It was bright and spacious, with a very elegant, gracious air about it. There were some interesting designer boutiques along the foyer, and Helena's steps slowed as her eye was caught by stunning dresses and then a jewellery shop, with gems that sparkled fiercely under display cabinet lighting.

The guard opened the door through to a large office, where Antonia was working at a computer. 'Visitor for Mr. Ainsley,' he announced, before departing abruptly.

Antonia looked up, startled. 'Helena, this is an unexpected visit.' The woman's expression was vaguely disapproving. 'You know Tate is a very busy man. He's up to his eyes getting ready for the opening of the hotel.'

'Well, it doesn't matter if he's too busy to see me,' Helena said with a shrug, hoping against hope that she could escape without seeing him.

'I'll tell him you're here.' The woman stood up. 'I

think he's down in the restaurant at the moment. I'll go find him.'

'Thanks.' Helena's eyes darted around the room as she was left alone. There was a door through to a connecting office. It was slightly ajar and she could see a large desk strewn with papers and files. Tate's private office?

Drawn irresistibly towards that desk, she pushed the door further open, her eyes swinging around the room with curiosity. It was a beautiful office, with spectacular views out across the bay, but it was the desk that held Helena's attention. There was a bright orange file lying on it…a file that looked just like the one Tate had brought to her father's house.

Casting a nervous glance behind her, in case Tate might suddenly appear, she crept quickly towards that file.

Her heart hammered unmercifully against her chest as she flicked it open and ran her eyes over the sheets of paper inside. There were rows of figures, projections of future profit and expenditure…but for what?

'Can I be of assistance?' Tate's coolly sardonic tone made her jump. She hadn't heard the outer door open. Guilt made colour flood to her face, and hastily she stepped back from the desk, cursing herself for being caught like this.

'I…I was just picking up some papers for you,' she mumbled awkwardly, looking over to where he was leaning nonchalantly against the doorframe, watching her. 'They…they had fallen on the floor.'

She could see by the dark expression on his face that he didn't believe her.

'Didn't anyone ever tell you that it's very rude to go through someone else's private papers?' His voice was dry, his eyes harsh for a moment as they raked over her slender figure.

'I wasn't going through them.' She angled her chin up. 'And anyway, if everything was above board you wouldn't mind someone reading through your paperwork.' She couldn't resist the dig. After all she wasn't the one who was trying to swindle someone...why should she feel like the guilty party?

'Meaning?' His eyes narrowed.

A tremor of alarm raced through her. Perhaps open confrontation was not a good idea, she thought hurriedly. At least not until she had something concrete to accuse him with. 'Meaning that I was merely picking up your papers for you.' She shrugged and tried to keep her voice nonchalant. 'What's the problem, Tate? You seem very defensive.'

'The problem is a very nosy little girl, with big green eyes, who likes to poke her button nose in where it's not wanted.' He strode across to her with a purposeful air about him, and she found herself backing away.

To her relief he merely closed the file with a firm hand.

'Is...is that the file you brought over to my father's house the other day?' She forced herself to ask the question, even though Tate's closeness and his manner were intimidating her slightly.

He turned to face her, and she suddenly found herself hemmed in against the window. 'Aren't you supposed to be on holiday?'

'What has that to do with anything?' She glanced up and met his eyes, and then promptly wished she hadn't. His gaze was more than a little unnerving.

For one heart-stopping moment she found herself remembering her dream last night...the seductive way he had looked at her, the wild, sweet feeling of longing. A wave of heat rushed through her body; she felt horrified...confused...almost dizzy with the torrent of emotions that dream had stirred up inside her.

'You should be thinking about pleasure, not business.' For a moment his eyes lingered on the softness of her lips. 'How about joining me for a drink out on the terrace?'

Was he deliberately trying to distract her from that file on his desk? She couldn't think straight while he was so close.

'Helena?' he prompted her with a frown, and she wondered if her face looked as hot as she felt.

Desperately she tried to think sensibly...first she needed to dismiss the memory of that dream—it was totally ridiculous. Secondly she shouldn't let him sidetrack her so easily. She needed to know what was in that file. What exactly he was up to where her father was concerned.

'I don't want a drink. I really just want to ask you about the business you're doing with my father.'

'You don't give up, do you?' he grated sardonically, and stepped back from her.

'Well, I'm worried about my father and I was hoping—'

'We'll talk out on the terrace.' He turned towards the door.

Feeling that maybe at last she might get some answers, she allowed him to lead her through to the outer office.

'Get someone to send a bottle of champagne out to the terrace, please, Antonia,' he said swiftly to his secretary on the way past.

Antonia looked aghast at him. 'But, sir, you've got an appointment in—'

'Take care of it for me, Tony, please.' Tate put a guiding arm at Helena's back as he moved out towards the reception area. 'Oh, and fix my desk, will you? Helena informed me that there were papers strewn all over the floor.'

Helena had a fleeting glimpse of Antonia's annoyed expression before Tate closed the door on her.

'I really don't want any champagne,' she murmured, feeling on edge again. Why was it that Tate wanted to turn everything into a social occasion?

'Nonsense—a glass of bubbly will do you good. You need to relax more, Helena.'

She didn't need to relax, she told herself crossly. What she needed was some straight answers, but it didn't look as if she was going to get any...not unless she pushed much more forcibly.

'So, am I to gather it is just concern for your father's business dealings that brings you over here today?' He opened doors through to a sumptuous lounge, where sliding glass doors led onto a terrace with a spectacular view of the beach. 'Or are you just curious to see this place?'

'Perhaps a little of both,' she admitted cautiously.

He nodded. 'And what do you think?'

'Think?' She glanced over at him blankly. She thought he was a scheming shark, but she could hardly say so.

'About the hotel?' A curve of a smile lit his features.

'Very impressive.' What else could she say? The place was beautiful. 'When do you open?'

'Friday.' He pulled out a chair for her at the edge of the terrace, so that she could sit overlooking the view.

'Actually, we are a little behind schedule. We should have opened last month, but you know how it is with builders and interior designers—there are always some last-minute hold-ups.'

Oh, yes. Helena knew what it was like when things got behind schedule. Banks started to scream for their money. Paying a loan on a place like this would be no joke. She turned speculative eyes on Tate. Had he over-stretched himself financially? If so, it would explain why he was leading her father astray. It would explain a lot of things—including his scathing remarks about the banking establishment.

'Anyway, I'm throwing a party to celebrate the opening on Friday night. I hope you will come?' Tate continued smoothly as he sat down beside her. 'Your father and Vivian will be attending.'

Her heart thudded uncomfortably. She certainly didn't feel like celebrating. And anyway it would prob-ably be a big affair, everyone would attend...Cass and Debby included.

'Thank you for the invitation, Tate, but I don't think I'll be able to make it,' she said politely, a hint of stiffness in her tone.

'Why not?' He turned blue eyes directly on her.

When he looked at her like that it really threw her. She swallowed hard and desperately tried to gather her thoughts. 'Well...because I'm doing something else on Friday.' She prayed that he wouldn't ask her what she was doing, but it was a forlorn hope because it was his very next question.

'I'm just...busy.' She couldn't think of a good ex-cuse, her mind was running in circles. But why should she have to give him a reason? she wondered angrily. He should just accept the fact that she couldn't make it. It shouldn't matter to him if she was there or not anyway.

'Has your refusal anything to do with the fact that David Cass and his fiancée will be attending?'

The coolly asked question made Helena's nerves snap. 'No...absolutely nothing... Why the hell do you keep mentioning that man's name to me?'

'Because you were once in love with him—'

'I was never in love with him.' Helena practically spat the words. 'And I just don't want to come to your damn party... I'm sorry if that sounds rude, but unfortunately you don't seem to be able to accept a polite refusal.'

'You are running away, Helena.' His words were spoken calmly, as if her heated outburst was of no consequence. 'You haven't got over Cass—that much is written all over you. The best thing you could do for yourself is face up to that fact...face up to him and then forget him.'

Shock waves flowed through her at that outrageous statement. 'Have you quite finished?' Her voice trembled with rage. 'How dare you lecture me on how I run my life? You don't know the first thing about me.'

'I know you've been hurt...I know you are still hurting.'

She glared at him, her green eyes glimmering with deep shock and hurt.

'Don't look at me like that,' he murmured softly. His gaze moved from the furious expression in her eyes to the gentle, vulnerable curve of her lips.

The way he was looking at her fired her fury even more...it disturbed her intensely, it made her think again about that dream...how she had willingly surrendered herself into his arms... Horrified, she thrust that thought aside.

'I don't want to upset you, Helena. But sometimes it helps to—'

'I don't need any kind of help, especially from you.' She cut across him in a bitterly angry tone. 'I couldn't give a damn about David Cass. I don't know why you're so intent on talking about the man. If I never heard his name mentioned again it would be a day too soon.'

With that she got up from the chair, her heart beating with wild anger and with a strange kind of sadness as well. Her emotions were in total chaos, and she couldn't begin to understand them or control them. There was a feeling deep within almost like grief, and that really threw her.

'Helena.' He got swiftly to his feet and caught her arm as she turned away.

'Helena, don't go—I'm sorry if I've upset you.'

She looked back at him reluctantly, the note of apology making her feel close to tears for some reason.

'You—' She didn't get a chance to say anything more, because suddenly and unexpectedly the hand on her arm tightened and he was pulling her back towards him. He must have caught her off balance, because she swayed against him. He put out a hand to steady her, and for a moment she was held close against his chest.

Shock held her immobilised for a second. She could feel the warmth of his body pressing against her, feel the beat of his heart through the thin material of her dress, smell the tangy scent of his cologne.

She pulled sharply back, her face suffused with wild

colour. 'I…I'm sorry…I lost my balance.' Her words were jerky, and she couldn't look him in the eye.

'It was my fault.' He reached out a hand and touched her chin, tipping her face up gently so that she had to look at him. The touch of his hand against the softness of her skin made her remember the way he had touched her in that dream. She flinched away. 'Don't, Tate… don't.'

'Sit down with me, Helena,' he invited soothingly. 'Let's start again…no mention of Cass.'

She looked at him then, and he held up both hands in a gesture of surrender. 'Promise,' he said smoothly.

She swallowed hard. She really just wanted to walk away…she hadn't wanted to be here in the first place. She couldn't understand this man…she should feel nothing but contempt for the way he was treating her father and yet…and yet he was capable of stirring up other strange emotions inside her. He seemed to have the knack of sending her reeling into turmoil with just a direct glance from those blue eyes. The knack of making her forget to ask the pointedly important questions she should be asking.

He pulled out her chair and looked at her enquiringly.

She nodded and sat back down, but she was only staying for her father's sake, she told herself forcibly. She owed it to Lawrence to try and find out what was going on here.

'Good.' Tate smiled soothingly. 'Let's have that champagne, shall we?' Without waiting for her answer, he marched down to the doors of the building behind them and shouted through for a waiter to attend to them.

Helena was glad of the respite; she needed a few moments to pull her scattered wits together.

'Antonia must have forgotten to relay my message,' Tate said with a grin when he returned to sit next to her. 'Hope the service is a bit better here when we finally open.'

'I'm sure that it will be,' Helena said absently. 'The staff are probably well aware of your high standards. Your reputation at the other hotel is second to none.'

'Yes, we've been very successful.'

Helena noticed wryly that the man wasn't in the slightest bit modest.

A waiter interrupted them, bringing a bottle of Moët et Chandon and two crystal champagne flutes on a silver tray. 'Sorry for the delay, sir,' he said nervously. 'Shall I open the bottle for you?'

Tate shook his head. 'Thanks, Jez.'

Helena watched Tate as he took the champagne from the ice-bucket and popped the cork with casual ease. This was the second bottle of champagne he had bought for her. Was Tate trying to lull her into a false sense of security with this show of generosity? If so, he had underestimated her.

'About your business dealings with my father,' she said suddenly.

'Don't you ever relax?' He spoke as if he was only half listening—his attention seemed to be on the frothy bubbles welling up in the glasses.

'I only want a few straight answers,' she whispered huskily.

Tate handed her the glass of champagne. 'I'll tell you exactly what is going on. I'm helping Lawrence to reverse his run of financial bad luck.'

'How, exactly?' With difficulty she didn't drop her

eyes from his, even though they felt as if they were burning into her.

He smiled suddenly, his eyes holding hers with a look of intent that made apprehension curl inside her. 'I'll tell you what,' he said slowly, contemplatively. 'You come to the opening party on Friday and I just might enlighten you.'

She frowned. 'Can't you just give me a straightforward answer?'

'No.' His voice was calmly composed, no hint of annoyance—or of any emotion, for that matter.

'I don't know why you're so damn keen for me to come to this party,' she countered furiously. Once again she felt that Tate was backing her into a corner. It was something he seemed very good at.

He shrugged. 'Everyone will be there…it will please Lawrence…it will please me.'

Helena's lips set in a line of disapproval. Obviously the fact that it would please her father was Tate's primary incentive.

Their eyes met, and Helena felt that tremor of apprehension dart through her again. Tate unnerved her totally…she didn't trust him…she didn't want to trust him.

'What can it hurt?' Tate asked nonchalantly.

Helena could have given him a hundred reasons…but she didn't dare voice one.

'I'll pick you up, say about—'

'No.' She interrupted him forcefully. 'If I come, I'll come with Pop and Vivian.'

He shrugged casually, but there was a flicker of triumph in the blue depths of his eyes.

CHAPTER SIX

HELENA stood in front of her bedroom mirror and surveyed her appearance. Against all her instincts she was dressed, ready to go to the opening party at the Bounty Hotel.

She had taken a lot of trouble with her appearance—her hair gleamed like highly polished mahogany, her make-up was subtle, highlighting her high cheekbones and the soft curve of her lips, and the turquoise halter-neck dress she wore skimmed her figure in a very sexy way, revealing a long length of her bare back burnished a soft honey-gold by the sun.

She hadn't paid as much attention to her appearance in a long time, but she was aware of a deep need to look her very best tonight. Not that she wanted to impress anybody, but she did need to give herself a vital boost of self-confidence.

The thought of seeing Cass and Debby again brought a chill to her heart. She just didn't know how she would handle it.

Of course, everyone thought that the reason Helena had fallen out with Debby had been jealousy. Everybody there tonight would nod and say, 'Poor Helena...still incredibly bitter, still carrying a torch for David Cass.' And Tate would be among those people. Her heart pounded uncomfortably.

Ironically it had been Tate all those years ago who

had told Helena that Cass had started seeing Debby. He had come over to the house to see Vivian and had found Helena sitting in the lounge, a look of abject unhappiness on her pale features. He had thought that she was nursing a broken heart—in fact she had still been reeling with shock from Cass's violent attack on her.

She remembered what Tate had said, each exact word, and the way he had watched her with that hooded expression in his deep blue eyes as they took in everything from the slender fragility of her figure to the paleness of her skin.

His eyes had lingered on the softness of her lips, the fierce glitter in her eyes. 'Cass certainly isn't worth your tears.'

The words had surprised her. Tate had barely known her—she'd been astounded that he'd even known she was seeing Cass. When she had said this to him he had shrugged, his manner nonchalant.

'Come on, Helena,' he had drawled softly. 'Barbados is a small island. I knew you were seeing the guy, and when I saw him kissing your friend the other day even I could put two and two together.'

Helena remembered the intense shock his words had stirred up inside her, she remembered the heart-wrenching twist, the anguish, the worry. 'Debby…he's seeing Debby?' Her face had drained of all colour, leaving her so white that her skin had looked like porcelain.

For a moment he had hesitated, a flicker of surprise in the deep blue of his eyes. 'I thought you knew.'

She hadn't answered, had turned tail and raced from the house. Her one thought to warn her friend about Cass.

It had never occurred to her that Debby wouldn't listen to her, that anything she said about Cass would be put down to jealousy. It had been the final bitter betrayal. She had known that if Debby didn't believe her, nobody would...

Her father's voice drifted upstairs, asking if she was ready. She reached for her bag, her nerves unbearably taut. The evening ahead suddenly seemed like an ordeal of torture.

The party was in full swing when they arrived. People filled the open air restaurant, and on the terrace beside the pool a steel band was playing a Caribbean calypso.

'It's a very good turn-out,' Vivian murmured, her eyes moving around the crowd. 'I see quite a few well-known celebrities, and some very prominent business people here.'

Helena couldn't bring herself to look too deeply into the mass of people, for fear of seeing Cass. Her heart was thumping wildly, and she hated herself for allowing such tension to invade her body.

Striving to behave normally, she took a glass of champagne from the tray of a passing waiter and tried very hard to concentrate on the conversation around her.

The night air was warm and tropical, scented with bougainvillaea and the exotic perfume from the long white tuberoses that grew in abundance in the gardens next to the coconut grove. Helena breathed deeply, willing herself to relax, to forget the past and David Cass—all that mattered was here and now.

'Glad you could make it.' The dulcet tones of Tate's deep voice drifted over the babble of voices.

'We wouldn't have missed it for the world.' Vivian's

eyes sparkled with vivid animation as she turned to reach and kiss their host.

'Lawrence.' Tate held his hand in a firm handshake. 'Good to see you.'

Helena found herself watching Tate with the strangest sensation in her chest. He looked so incredibly attractive that for just a moment her eyes were locked on him with complete fascination—a fascination that made her forget her unease and her surroundings.

He was wearing a white dinner jacket that emphasised his dark tan and the darkness of his hair. It also drew attention to the forceful breadth of his shoulders. He looked like a movie star, the kind of man a woman fantasised over...longed for in her bed. The thought shocked Helena. She had never longed for any man— and she certainly wasn't going to start with a man like Tate Ainsley.

As his head turned to look towards her she quickly held out her hand, in case he moved to greet her the way he had greeted Vivian. She didn't want him to kiss her, couldn't bear for him to come too close.

If he found her formality amusing it didn't show in the dark gleam of his eyes. He took her hand in a firm grasp and shook it in a very businesslike way. 'Helena, you look incredibly beautiful.' There was nothing businesslike about the tone of his voice, or the look in his eyes as they drifted over the fragile curves of her slender figure.

Helena had to remind herself very forcibly that the compliment was probably for Lawrence's benefit—that the only reason he had invited her in the first place was to please her father.

'You're too kind.' Her voice held the merest hint of

sarcasm as she smiled coolly up at him whilst extricating the hand that he was still holding.

'It's a good turn-out, Tate,' Lawrence said in a friendly tone. 'It's a credit to you—just like the Ainsley Hotel.'

'Yes, not bad.' Tate nodded, and turned slightly away from Helena.

For a while the conversation centred around the hotel, then Tate turned back towards her suddenly. 'How about a dance, Helena?' he asked nonchalantly, indicating the dance-floor where some couples were swaying to a low, romantic ballad being given a Caribbean flavour by the steel band.

She shook her head. 'No, thanks, Tate. I...I don't dance.' The thought of being held so close by Tate Ainsley made her heart thud most uncomfortably.

'I'll teach you.' He reached for her hand.

'Tate, I really don't dance.' She hid her hands behind her back, a note of panic clear in her tone.

'Everyone dances.' He wasn't about to take no for an answer, that much was clear from his tone, from the direct light in those disturbing blue eyes.

She sighed and shrugged slender shoulders. 'Well, if I must,' she said, making it clear that she was accepting the offer grudgingly. She didn't want her father getting the wrong idea about them.

Even so, as Tate caught hold of her arm she caught the gleam of satisfaction in her father's eye. 'You know, my father seems to think you are sainted,' she said sarcastically as they walked down the steps towards the dance-floor. 'Why do you think that is?'

He slanted a wry glance down at her. 'My angelic looks?' he asked, with a lift of one eyebrow. 'Or maybe he just likes the fact that I'm well able to handle his wayward daughter?'

'Wayward?' She glared at him furiously. 'I am not wayward. I'll have you know I have never given my father a moment's trouble.'

'No?' He looked amused by that. 'Well, maybe you've got it wrong, and you're the one who is sainted.'

'I didn't say that,' she muttered in irritation. 'And for your information you are not able to ''handle'' me, as you so quaintly put it.'

'Was I being quaint?' He led her into the centre of the dance-floor and then turned to face her. 'That was never my intention,' he said with a grin. 'But as for ''handling'' you, now that was definitely foremost in my mind.' He reached to put his hands on her shoulders, moving her closer to him.

Helena wanted to pull away forcibly, but she was conscious of people watching them, and she didn't want to make a scene.

'Have I told you how beautiful you look tonight?' He murmured the words in a low tone that was somehow very seductive.

She tried to hold herself away from him, to hold her mind aloof from the charm he could turn on so well. 'I believe you've done the compliment bit,' she grated drolly.

'You know, when you get angry your eyes go a deep emerald colour...they are very bewitching.' He spoke softly, totally ignoring her frosty manner.

She swallowed hard. She wasn't going to be taken in by this suave smooth-talker, she told herself vehemently...she just wasn't.

'Talking about emeralds,' she said coolly. 'What do

you know about a certain mine that my father is investing in?' She slanted her head to look up at him.

'Quite a lot.' He smiled down at her, his eyes moving over the smooth oval of her face, lingering on the full softness of her lips. 'But I don't want to talk about it now.'

She looked away from him, disconcerted by the sudden surge of emotion that seemed to be racing through her body, sparked off purely from the way he had looked at her mouth. Her heart slammed furiously against her breast as she said stiffly, 'You know I only agreed to come here tonight because I want you to explain your business dealings with my father.'

As she spoke she tried to concentrate on keeping her body slightly apart from his, but it was extremely difficult because the floor was packed with people and Tate's arms were strong and protective in case someone steered into them.

'You must be one hell of an asset to the bank, my girl, because you've got a one-track mind.'

'I'm not your girl.' She breathed the words with fiery indignation.

'Shouldn't we be a little closer?' He ignored her words, her tone of voice, and boldly moved his hands from her shoulders to her waist. His head lowered, so that his cheek touched against the softness of her hair as he spoke in a low, husky voice. 'That way I can whisper about liquid assets in your ear.'

'You are totally infuriating, do you know that?' She tried very hard to ignore the shiver that raced down her spine at his closeness.

Being held so close against him made her senses spin. His body felt warm against hers, warm and vital somehow. She wondered if he could feel how heavily her heart was slamming against her chest.

'I thought you said you couldn't dance?'

That husky whisper did very strange things to her blood pressure. This wasn't dancing. It was more a slow, seductive movement that managed to obscure the music and the crowds in a haze of wild mixed-up sounds and shadowy images.

'I…I thought you were going to whisper about liquid assets?' She tried very hard to play him at his own game. Every time he changed the subject away from business she was going to change it right back, she told herself determinedly. She wasn't going to give up until she got some answers from Tate Ainsley.

'OK, first asset is a dark-haired, beautiful daughter.' He growled the words in a teasing way. 'And if I was an asset stripper—'

'Tate, a joke is a joke, but you are going too far!' Helena's breath caught, and she tried to take a step back. The result was quite the opposite. Tate's arms just tightened around her and she was pressed so close against his chest that she could feel the warm naked skin beneath the fine material of his shirt.

'Sorry, Helena. You're right—we shouldn't be talking business.' He drawled the words seductively, teasingly. 'You seem to bring out a very crazy streak in me. I can't seem to concentrate on anything but how you look tonight.'

A shiver raced through her slender figure. She knew he was just winding her up, that he didn't mean a word he was saying, yet her skin prickled with intense awareness as his breath fanned softly against the soft, vulnerable curve of her neck.

She tried very hard to formulate some light-hearted

reply, but her mind wouldn't function properly. Her stomach clenched with a very strange sensation, almost like diving from a great height into the sea. Breathtaking, frightening, exhilarating... She couldn't understand those emotions...couldn't seem to think straight...

Being in his arms was so strange... She should hate it... She didn't trust this man; he was ruthless, everything she despised, and yet...and yet the strangest sensations were welling through her. Panic rose, and she pushed against his shoulder.

'I've...I've had enough, Tate.' Her voice held that ring of anguish...that uncertain, almost little-girl sound. 'I want to stop now.'

To her surprise he released her immediately. He looked down at her, his eyes serious as they raked over the smooth beauty of her face, taking in the over-bright glimmer of her green eyes. 'OK...I could do with a drink anyway,' he said easily.

She swallowed hard, because perversely, now that he had pulled away, she wanted to feel his arms around her again. She frowned, totally mixed up, hating herself for the emotional mishmash of her thoughts. What was wrong with her? she wondered, almost hysterically. She was usually so in control. No one had ever stirred her to such a fever-pitch of conflicting responses.

The crowds around them on the dance-floor had increased, and it was a struggle to get to the edge. A woman caught hold of Tate's sleeve. Looking around, Helena saw that it was Antonia. The other woman looked extremely glamorous in a very short mini-dress that clung to her beautiful figure alluringly.

'Just wanted to congratulate you, Tate,' she purred, looking up at him with open adoration in her eyes. 'The opening is a tremendous success—everyone is thoroughly enjoying it.'

'Thanks, Tony.' Tate smiled down at her. 'And thanks for all the hard work you've put in over the last few weeks. I've appreciated it.'

The girl's cheeks flushed with pleasure. 'Perhaps we could have a dance later...?' she suggested, sending him a coy look from under her lashes.

Tate nodded. 'Perhaps,' he said easily.

The girl's face fell; obviously she had expected Tate to take her up on the suggestion right away.

It suddenly occurred to Helena in that moment that Antonia wasn't just infatuated with Tate, she was in love with him.

Helena's eyes moved to Tate—he was smiling gently at the girl. Was Tate attracted to Antonia? Her heart skipped a beat at the thought. Not that she cared, she told herself heatedly...she couldn't give a damn.

Antonia turned slightly, and her eyes caught on Helena. 'Hello, I didn't see you there.' Her smile was cool. 'There's an old friend of yours at the buffet bar, you know. I was just speaking to him.'

'Oh?' Helena hoped that her skin didn't look as pale as it felt, because for a moment she felt as if all her colour was draining away from her complexion as she waited for Cass's name to be mentioned.

'Rupert Law... He was your old boss when you worked here at the bank, wasn't he?' Antonia continued smoothly.

'Oh...oh, yes.' Somehow she gathered herself together, relief heady. Rupert Law had been manager at the main bank in Bridgetown for years. He was a very pleasant man with a very astute business head, and Helena had enjoyed working for him. She was also very grateful to him, because when she had decided to leave Barbados he had been the person who had helped her to get such a fabulous job in London.

'Thought so.' Antonia nodded. 'And Debby is just behind you at the mini-bar.' The woman's eyes flashed fire. 'Why don't you go over and say hello? I'm sure she would love to see you again...'

Helena felt ill. She couldn't even pretend to look around. There was a cold, clammy sensation in the pit of her stomach.

'Shall I call her over?' Antonia enquired in a sweetly innocent tone.

Despite the heat of the night a chill raced through her. Stricken with fear, she lifted her eyes towards Tate. She was unaware of how vulnerable she looked in that moment. Her eyes were wide and they glowed a deep emerald-green, almost like a wild animal's, trapped in a beam of heavy light.

'Helena has a lot of catching up to do with many people here tonight, Tony,' Tate interrupted smoothly, and casually he stretched an arm across Helena's shoulder.

Surprisingly Helena found the gesture comforting; it was like a protective barrier against the sudden coldness that had closed around her on hearing that Debby was standing just behind her. If Deborah was there Cass would be there also... She shivered, and Tate's arm tightened reassuringly.

'We'll stroll over and say hello to Debby in a moment.'

Tate made it sound as if they were a couple, but in that instant Helena couldn't have cared less how it sounded—she was just grateful to be helped out of this emotional mire. No matter what Tate said, she had no intention of strolling over to say hello to Cass.

'Do me a favour, Tony, will you?' Tate smiled coldly. 'Just pop through to the kitchens and make sure everything is running smoothly in there.'

To say that Antonia looked annoyed would have been an understatement. Her beautiful features clouded sulkily, but she said nothing, just turned to do as he'd asked.

'Antonia is an attractive woman, but she's not the most subtle of creatures, is she?' he enquired, raising one eyebrow in lazy amusement.

She tried to return his smile, tried to make light of the incident, as if she really didn't care, but she couldn't think of anything light-hearted to say and her smile was decidedly wobbly.

Tate pulled her close in against his side, and his hand rubbed the bare skin of her arm in a light, comforting way. Helena leaned against him. She despised herself for her weakness but she was intensely glad of his warmth, his presence.

'You know what I think?' he said lightly, his dark eyes roving over the pallor of her face. 'I think you should just turn around with me now and say a casual hello to Debby. Get it over with, Helena, and then just forget about her...about Cass.'

Despite the warmth of the evening, Helena could feel herself growing colder and colder with each word that Tate spoke.

'Face up to your demons, Helena.' His voice was a lightly encouraging whisper. 'I'm right by your side and I won't let you down.'

She swallowed hard. 'I...I can't.'

'No such word as "can't", and it's better to do it

now. I won't prolong the agony—a few quick words and we can turn away and you can relax.'

Helena chanced a brief look behind her, her heart thumping rapidly. She saw Debby immediately. She was surrounded by a group of people that Helena didn't know. Cass was not among them.

For just a moment Helena's eyes rested on the girl who had been her closest friend. She didn't look very different. She still had that attractive blonde bob, the same clear skin and lovely brown eyes. The only change was the rather serious expression on her pretty features. Helena looked hurriedly away.

'You used to be such good friends,' Tate said gently. 'It can't hurt to say hello.'

'No, Tate.' She pulled away from him firmly, an expression of determination on her face. She didn't want to see Cass or Deborah ever again. She wanted to forget that they existed.

At that moment a group of people came over to congratulate Tate on the party. Helena seized the opportunity to escape from the situation and moved blindly away through the crowds.

Her heart was pounding so loudly that it was filling her eardrums painfully. She needed to get away from here, she thought desperately. She needed to sort out her father's affairs and fly straight back to London, away from all of this.

A cool waft of air swept over her as she stepped through the swing doors of the hotel. It was like a tranquil haven inside the main foyer. Cool, silent, not a person in sight. She immediately felt better.

For a moment she found herself remembering the reassurance of Tate's arm around her, the gentle note in his voice. He had sounded as if he'd genuinely wanted to help her face up to Debby and Cass—he had sounded so concerned.

She swallowed hard. Tate was concerned about himself, nothing else. He was a con man, a rogue. Or was he? a little voice asked her, deep inside. Where was her proof?

Her eyes moved over the thickly carpeted foyer towards the reception desk. Surprisingly there was no one on duty—obviously everyone was outside enjoying the party. Her gaze centred on the door which led through to Tate's office and she found herself remembering the file she had seen in there the other day...the document her father had signed without even reading...

If only she had managed to study those papers before Tate had interrupted her she might have found all the answers to her questions. Her lips tightened as she remembered Tate's earlier teasing remarks about asset-stripping. If she was waiting for him to shed some light on his business dealings with her father she would be in Barbados forever.

Would Tate's office be locked? she wondered suddenly. Disregarding any feelings of apprehension, she headed down the corridor, a light of determination in her green eyes. There was only one way to find out, and she seriously needed to see those files.

When the door through to the office swung open she almost expected alarm bells to ring or a hand to clamp down on her shoulder. Nothing happened. Her heart thumping uneasily, she slipped quietly into the darkened room and across to the inner office. That, too, was amazingly unlocked.

She stumbled a little in the dark, until her eyes started to adjust and she could see well enough to put on the desk-lamp.

Unlike on her previous visit, the desk was now clear. Helena turned her attention to the filing cabinet. Her hand trembled slightly as she reached out to see if it was locked. The only sound in the silence of the room was the rapid beat of her heart.

She moistened her lips nervously, her hand tightening around the handle. She wasn't doing anything dishonest, she told herself reassuringly. All she wanted was the truth.

When the drawer slid open Helena could hardly believe her luck. But the ecstatic feeling of triumph was short-lived. The very next moment the door opened behind her.

Panic made her whirl around unsteadily. She fully expected to see Tate standing in the doorway. It was a wild shock when instead she found herself eye to eye with David Cass.

CHAPTER SEVEN

HELENA remembered everything about Cass in that instant. How his smile never quite reached the grey of his eyes. How carefully he cultivated the immaculate image of the charming ladies' man.

In looks he hadn't changed one bit, but Helena saw him through different eyes now. His thick blond hair was cut in a structured way, so that it sat in smooth, perfect lines, and a piece fell onto his forehead in a way that looked casual but in fact was anything but... Helena knew that he had probably spent an hour getting it to look like that.

His face was hard-boned and leanly attractive. Helena noticed that the lips she had once thought of as sensuous had in fact got a slightly cruel curve. Oh, yes, she could see David Cass clearly for what he was... Helena's heart beat ferociously against her chest. She alone knew the real Cass.

'What...what are you doing in here?' From somewhere she regained a modicum of composure, but it was hard—unbearably hard.

'I was about to ask you the same question.' He was very relaxed, a gleam of amusement playing around his lips. 'I saw you leave the party and I thought I'd follow you...renew our acquaintance.'

Her hand shook uncontrollably as she pushed the file drawer closed with a sharp, angry action. 'You've got a barefaced nerve, Cass.' She hissed the words, her eyes burning with fury.

'Aren't you pleased to see me?' He drawled the words coolly, an edge of sarcasm rasping beneath the surface. 'I only wanted to tell you how beautiful you are looking.' His eyes raked over her body, and she flinched as if he had struck her. 'When I saw you on the dance-floor with Tate I could hardly believe my eyes. You always were incredibly sensual...but now—'

'Stop it.' She started to back away from him as he came closer. 'Keep away from me, Cass, or I swear, I'll—'

'You'll what?' he grated contemptuously. 'Tell everyone what a big bad wolf I am? I suppose you're leading poor old Tate a merry dance, just as you did me.'

Helena couldn't find her voice to answer, her body was frozen with terror.

'I'll have to have words with him—tell him that all he needs is a firm hand.' He laughed then, and the sound was so reminiscent of the nightmares she had lived through for so long that it filled her with cold fear.

He reached out towards her and she stepped back, only to find herself wedged against the desk.

'Darling Helena—'

The overhead light blazed on suddenly, interrupting his sentence, making her blink.

'I hate to interrupt such a cosy scene—' a cool voice cut the air, making Cass drop his arm and look around in surprise '—but you are in my office.'

Tate was standing in the doorway, his eyes narrowed as they took in the closeness of their stance. 'If you wanted a passionate reunion you should have booked a bedroom, Cass.'

Helena's relief changed to fury, and her eyes flew to Tate's face. 'How dare you say something like that?' Her voice grated unsteadily in the tense silence of the room. She sounded breathless, emotionally charged.

Tate's eyes moved over the pallor of her skin, the bright blaze of her eyes, then he switched his attention coolly to Cass. 'How dare you barge into my office?' His voice was low, yet his anger was evident in the controlled tone, in the way he was looking at the other man.

For a moment there was a flicker of unease in Cass's cool grey eyes. Then he pulled that mantle of flippant charm down around him. 'Sorry, old chap.' He moved back from Helena. 'Just saw Helena come in here and thought I'd say hello... No harm done.'

The light-hearted words had no effect on the cool expression on Tate's features. 'That's a matter of opinion, isn't it?' he drawled silkily. Then he looked towards Helena. 'What's your excuse...a little late-night tidying? Picking up some papers from the floor... dusting?'

'Don't be ridiculous.' Her voice was raw, her heart slamming furiously against her chest. All she wanted to do was run as far away as she possibly could. This was a nightmare...an absolute nightmare.

'Well, if you will excuse me.' Cass sidled cautiously towards the door. 'Debby will be wondering where I've got to.'

'Pity you didn't think about that before.' Tate's manner was unrelenting.

'Yes...well...' Looking most uncomfortable, Cass reached the door.

If Helena hadn't been so shattered by the whole episode she might have enjoyed the look of alarm on
David Cass's face. But all she could think about was
what might have happened if Tate hadn't come into the
room when he had. Her heart thudded unsteadily.

Tate allowed Cass to leave, and silence fell on the
room. Helena sank back against the desk, her legs decidedly shaky.

'So?' Tate glared at her, his eyes hard. 'What *is* your
excuse?'

'For heaven's sake!' She shook her head, her eyes
clouding, her lips trembling with reaction. 'Just leave
it.'

He came further into the room. 'Did you plan to
meet Cass in here? Was it some kind of clandestine
arrangement?'

'Give me a break, Tate.'

He came even closer. 'No wonder you didn't want
to look Debby in the eye. To think that I bought that
vulnerable-little-girl act, and all the time you had arranged to meet Cass behind Debby's back—'

'I did no such thing.' Her voice blazed across his.

'So what was going on in here, then?'

She tried to ignore the steely warning in his voice
and remained silent, staring down at the floor, trying
desperately to get her emotions under some kind of
control.

'What was going on?' Tate reached out a hand and
jerked her chin upwards, forcing her to meet his eyes.

He looked furious. She had known he would be angry if he caught her snooping around his office again,
but she hadn't expected this kind of fury.

'Nothing.' She tried very hard to keep her voice
steady. 'I came in here because…' She swallowed hard,

before admitting the truth huskily. 'I needed to see that document my father signed. I'm desperately worried about him, Tate, and I wanted to put my mind at rest.'

'And Cass came to help you rake through the accounts, did he?' Tate's voice was harsh.

'No...no, of course not. Cass must have followed me. He just suddenly appeared.' Her voice trembled with reaction. 'I certainly didn't plan to meet him.'

'You're still in love with Cass, aren't you?' He moved back from her.

The quietly asked question made her heart crash against her chest. Her eyes flickered away from his. 'I was never in love with Cass. I told you that before.'

'You've told me a number of things before,' Tate responded sardonically. 'You told me you were picking papers up off the floor the other day, when it was quite obvious even to me that you were meddling.'

'Look, I apologise for intruding on your private affairs.' She stood up from the desk, her manner agitated, angry. 'But I've tried asking you about the business you are conducting with my father again and again, and you never give me a straight answer.'

'Perhaps because it's none of your damn business,' he said calmly. 'Have you stopped to consider that possibility at all?'

'Don't be so damned facetious.' Her green eyes flew towards his face. 'We are talking about my father, here...my home—'

'What has your home to do with anything?' he asked calmly.

'Well, Beaumont House has been in the family for generations...I'm certainly not going to stand back and watch while my father loses it.'

'You haven't much faith in Lawrence's business abilities, have you?' he asked drily.

'I...I used to have.' Her eyes narrowed on his face. 'But now he's all but given away my mother's land to you, plus he is selling everything he can get his hands on.'

'It's called raising capital,' Tate told her sardonically. 'And I can assure you that your father hasn't given anything away.'

'Well, Paul seems to think he has.' Helena glared at him. 'Paul is worried sick.'

'I'm sure he is,' Tate said wryly. 'Is that what has set you off on this desperate search through my papers? Is all this concern down to things that Paul has been saying?'

'Well...partly,' she admitted cautiously. She had probably already said too much. It had never been her intention to accuse Tate openly. Forewarned was forearmed, as her father used to say.

'Well, let me tell you a thing or two about your precious brother.' Tate came closer towards her in a threatening manner.

'I already know your thoughts on my brother.' She backed anxiously away from him.

'Number one, the only thing Paul is concerned about is himself,' Tate continued, as if she hadn't spoken. 'Number two, he doesn't understand one thing about business—'

'I know Paul isn't a businessman, but he does care about Pop,' Helena cut across him angrily.

'No, he doesn't, Helena. The only thing that Paul cares about is the fact that Lawrence has stopped paying him his allowance, and now your brother has to be serious about working for the first time in his life.'

Helena stared at Tate, her heart pounding with apprehension. 'I don't believe that.' She shook her head. 'Paul is concerned for my father…nothing else. What do you know about Paul's allowance anyway?'

'Plenty, as a matter of fact,' Tate answered her calmly. 'I helped your father when he was going through his accounts trying to raise capital. One of the first things I suggested he did was to stop Paul's allowance.'

'I see.' For a moment she was totally thrown by this piece of news. She hadn't even known that Paul was still receiving an allowance from her father!

Was that his reason for taking so vehemently against Tate? Had he brought her back to Barbados on a fool's errand? Trying to make her stir things between her father and Tate in the hope that he would get his allowance back? Surely not! Her heart sank. Surely Paul wouldn't sink so low as to make such seriously false accusations?

'And why did my father get you to go through his accounts?' She tried to dismiss the notion of Paul being so weak, and think clearly about Tate's involvement.

'Maybe because he trusted me?' Tate suggested in a low tone. Then he reached out and touched the side of her face. 'Which is more than you do, isn't it, Helena?'

The brush of his fingers against her skin made a shiver race right through her body.

'You look at me and think about Black Jack, don't you?' His hand moved to tilt her chin upwards, forcing her to look into the bright blue of his eyes.

'No…' Her voice trembled slightly, she felt breathless suddenly. His closeness was completely unnerving.

'But you do,' he insisted silkily. 'You think that I'm just like Black Jack Ainsley, only I lure poor, unsuspecting souls onto the jagged rocks of bankruptcy instead of into watery graves.' There was an edge of derision in his voice.

'No…no, of course not.' Even as she denied his accusations her creamy skin flared with telling colour. He was so accurate that it was embarrassing.

'Did you know that there was never any conclusive proof that Black Jack was guilty of those crimes?' he rasped harshly. 'But they hung him anyway…and that's what you are doing to me, Helena. Hanging me without evidence, without proof, without any reasonable grounds.'

'I'm not.' She shook her head furiously. 'I just—'

'You just suspect me anyway,' he cut across her grimly. 'Perhaps it's safer to assume my guilt…it helps you hide away from me.'

The sharp accusations came at her too quickly. They confused her, they wove through her mind planting seeds of doubt, overturning the rigid structures of her thoughts and sending waves of panic through her. 'I don't know what you're talking about.' Her voice sounded distraught. Suddenly she felt afraid, and her mind refused to probe too deeply.

His eyes raked knowingly over her face. 'Poor darling Helena,' he drawled softly, noting every flicker, every nuance of her expression. 'You're just not a very good judge of a man's character, are you?'

'Don't call me darling.' She ground the words out unsteadily. His accusation had touched on a raw nerve. After Cass she had doubted her judgement of men… still did.

'That's a privilege only reserved for Cass, is it?' he asked with aridity, his eyes narrowing on her face.

The colour of her skin changed from pink to scalding

red as she realised he must have heard Cass's words just before he entered the room.

'I noticed you didn't complain when he used the endearment.'

'It...it wasn't used in that way.' She stumbled over the explanation, her voice low and unsteady as she remembered those terrifying few moments before Tate had come in.

'How long are you going to carry a torch for that idiot?' Tate asked now in an angry tone.

'Carry a torch—?' She glared up at him. 'Let me tell you something, Tate Ainsley. I hate David Cass.' She spoke the words vehemently, her eyes glittering with fervent emotion. 'Hate him with everything inside me.'

'Sure.' Tate drawled the word sarcastically. 'You hate him so much that he would only have to crook his little finger and you'd be running back into his arms...and his bed, no doubt.'

White-hot rage gripped Helena at those words. They came at a moment when she was feeling confused and intensely vulnerable, and they were enough to tip her control over the edge.

Without thinking, she raised her hand and slapped him hard across the side of his face.

There was a moment of silence, time for Helena to regret the action as she saw Tate's face darken with fury.

'You little vixen.' He muttered the words under his breath.

Seeing the anger on Tate's face and hearing it in his voice made a tremor of alarm race through her. 'I'm sorry, Tate,' she said hastily. 'You...you shouldn't have said those things to me.'

He reached out towards her, and she stepped away

from him as fear instinctively took over. 'Don't...
please don't hurt me.'

'Hurt you?' He frowned. 'Helena, I—' He stepped
nearer as he spoke, but she was too terrified to listen.
She turned to try and escape from him across the room.

She didn't get very far. He caught her before she
could take more than a step and pulled her round to
face him.

'Helena, stop it!'

He spoke firmly. But still his voice barely penetrated
the mists of her fear.

'Helena, I'm not going to hurt you.' He caught hold
of her shoulders but his hands were gentle, as was the
tone of his voice as he murmured, 'You're safe with
me.'

Her heartbeats thundered in her ears; images flashed
through her mind—images of Cass, images of how he
had held her down on that night long ago, his voice
full of fury and loathing, his hands tearing at her cloth-
ing.

It took a moment to focus her eyes on Tate, to hear
what he was saying. She seemed literally to be in a
blind panic.

'Helena, I'm not going to hurt you.' Tate reiterated
the words, his hands gentle on her shoulders, his eyes
deeply concerned as they took in the white, almost
transparent look to her face.

She struggled to gather herself together, then as the
fear slowly receded it was replaced by shame. She bent
her face from Tate's probing stare. She couldn't look
at him.

What must he think of her? she wondered wildly.
Probably that she was one crazy woman. She couldn't

blame him either; she had totally overreacted, had gone completely to pieces.

'What was all that about?' His voice was gentle, with no hint of censure.

'I…I don't know. I just thought…' Her voice trailed off. How could she tell him that she had been frightened to death? How could she explain about Cass? He wouldn't believe her anyway…no one would.

'Helena?' He touched the side of her face. 'Helena, look at me.'

It took all of Helena's strength to raise her eyes to his. She felt such a fool—she felt as if she was hanging on to control by a thread.

'You know I wouldn't do anything to hurt you.' His thumb rubbed gently against her skin. 'That would never be my style…' His voice dipped teasingly. 'No matter how hard you slapped me.'

She tried to smile, but it was a tremulous one.

'Are you all right now?'

She nodded, unable to find her voice in case she broke down in front of him. That would be the final humiliating straw.

'I don't like to see you so upset.' His voice was tender, like the tone used for a cherished child. It made a curl of warmth stir deep within her.

His gaze moved over her pale skin and glimmering wide green eyes and then his arms went around her, drawing her close into their protective warmth.

For a moment surprise held her rigid against his chest. His hand stroked her back soothingly, comfortingly. 'I'm sorry I frightened you.' He spoke in a husky, reassuring tone, and she felt herself starting to relax.

It was good being held so close. Her heartbeats

started to slow to a steady beat as her breathing began to return to normal.

She could smell the familiar aroma of his cologne, hear his heart beating through the silk of his shirt. It was the strangest feeling—as if she was where she belonged. As if she had come home.

She frowned and thought that perhaps she should pull away from him, but she was extremely loath to listen to the voice of reason. She liked being where she was.

He was the one to pull away from her, holding her slightly away from him so that he could see her face. 'Feel better?'

She nodded. The fear had definitely gone, had been replaced by a much stranger emotion—one that Helena hadn't felt for a long, long time. She wanted to be back in the circle of his arms. She wanted to feel his body pressed against hers. She wanted him to kiss her. The idea was so strong that for a moment her eyes rested almost longingly on his lips. Then she looked up into his eyes.

Silence fell between them, and then suddenly there seemed to be an electric current of desire between them.

'Helena?' His voice was a mere whisper.

She closed her eyes as his head lowered towards her, and then his lips touched hers, gently, tentatively at first.

At first she didn't respond to him, just felt his lips move over the softness of hers with the skilled ease of a practised lover. Her heart thudded heavily against her chest. She felt as if something inside her was melting slowly, sending hot and cold shivers down into her very soul.

Then the kiss moved from gentle to hungry, and suddenly she was kissing him back with a passion that startled her so much that she pulled away from him in shock.

'Tate, I'm sorry.' Her breathing escaped in a rush. She put the back of her hand to her mouth in an instinctual gesture, pressing it to her lips as if to seal in the heat of his kiss. She raised uncertain eyes to his, and when she found him watching her with close attention she dropped her hand awkwardly to her side and stepped away from him, feeling embarrassed, confused.

'That…that should never have happened!' She muttered the words awkwardly, waiting for his reaction with a kind of breathless nervous anticipation.

His lips curved into a slow smile. 'I wouldn't say that,' he murmured gently.

'It…it was wrong…it was a mistake,' she insisted, yet her voice sounded most unconvincing.

He smiled, his eyes moving over her in a curiously tender way. 'If you say so.'

'I'll have to go, Tate.' She turned away from him. 'I'm afraid I can't face anyone at the party. I'm too…too—'

'Overwrought?' He supplied the word gently. 'Come on, I'll take you home.'

'What about your guests?' She flicked him an uncertain look.

'I'm tempted to say to hell with my guests.' He smiled at her lazily, in a way that did very strange things to her heartbeats. 'But I can't. I'll drop you off and I'll have to come straight back.'

The journey back to Beaumont House was made in virtual silence. Helena was grateful that Tate didn't try to strike up a conversation. She felt so confused by the emotions racing around inside her. Every time she thought about the way Tate had kissed her a sharp wave of heat swept through her.

'Will you be all right going into the house on your own?' Tate asked as he pulled the car up the long drive towards her house.

She nodded. 'Yes…thank you.'

As he pulled to a halt he turned to look at her. 'Why were you so afraid of me in the office?' He asked the question quietly. 'Why such terror?'

It was the question that she had been dreading. She knew he must be wondering why she had overreacted so terribly. She shrugged. 'I guess I just panicked. I knew I shouldn't have lashed out at you like that…and you…you looked so angry.' It was a lame excuse for such a strong reaction, but it was the best she could do.

She could tell from the expression on his face that he knew there was more to it than that. 'If you need someone to talk to I'm a good listener,' he said, in a low, understanding tone.

'Thanks, Tate, but there's nothing to talk about,' she said breathlessly. She couldn't begin to tell him about Cass…couldn't bear to admit she had been such a fool. 'I…I just overreacted—I'm a bit overtired, that's all.'

'Probably all that delving through my papers,' Tate said with dry humour.

'Yes, well.' She shrugged self-consciously. 'I have apologised for that…I was worried about Pop.'

'Well, stop worrying.' Tate's voice was calm and confident. 'Your father's finances are in good shape.

You can stop listening to Paul and take my word for it.'

Was he telling the truth? Helena's eyes moved over his ruggedly handsome features. Part of her very much wanted to take him at his word.

'All right?' He looked at her questioningly.

She hesitated, and then just nodded. She couldn't say the words because she just wasn't sure…she just didn't know what to believe any more.

'Good.' He smiled—a much more relaxed smile. 'It's all a question of trust, isn't it?'

'A question of trust.' The words played tantalisingly through her mind. It was indeed a matter of trust…but who to trust? That was the question. It was Paul's word against Tate's. She had no proof to support either man's accusations.

Her gaze moved over the hard, rugged planes of Tate's face. She remembered how he had kissed her, how he had held her so tenderly in his arms, and her heart flipped wildly. At this moment she knew who she wanted to believe…who she wanted to trust…and it wasn't her brother.

She reached for the doorhandle, annoyed with herself. She wasn't thinking rationally at all.

'Can I see you tomorrow, Helena?'

The softly spoken request took her by surprise.

'I could bring Gypsy over and we could go riding.'

She met the deep blue gaze and her lips curved in a warm instinctual smile. Paul would be most disappointed with her, she thought lazily, because she really didn't want to refuse that invitation at all.

CHAPTER EIGHT

'Is it true?' Helena held her breath as she waited for her brother's answer.

Paul's expression darkened ominously. 'I can't believe you've asked me to come over here just to accuse me like this.' His voice was low and bitter. 'I just can't believe it.'

'You haven't answered me.' Helena's voice was low and calm. 'Have you made up all these accusations about Tate just because your allowance has been stopped—?'

'No, you answer me this,' he ground across her vehemently. 'Have you taken Tate's side against me for purely rational, sensible reasons?' His eyes flicked over her slender figure in the beige jodhpurs and cream T-shirt contemptuously. 'I suppose you are seeing him today?'

He held up his hand as she started to speak. 'Don't try to make any excuses, Helena. I've got the general idea. You've obviously fallen for the guy and believe every charming word he speaks... Well, more fool you.' With that he turned and marched out of her bedroom, banging the door loudly behind him.

Helena flinched at the sound, at the violence of his outburst, and sat down at the dressing-table, her legs suddenly weak.

She heard the front door banging with equal force as her brother stormed from the house.

What a mess! For a moment Helena buried her head in her hands. She had hoped that by inviting Paul over here today she could come closer to the truth. It had been a large mistake. All she had succeeded in doing was upsetting her brother.

Was accepting Tate's invitation to go riding a mistake as well? She had tried not to examine her reasons too closely this morning. Had tried to tell herself that it was just a casual outing. She had even managed to persuade herself of that fact until Paul had arrived a few minutes ago. Now the doubts were back in force. She still didn't know whether to believe Tate or her brother.

She just didn't know what to do. She had tried to talk to her father this morning, but he had looked so tired and drawn that she hadn't had the heart to question him about anything.

Perhaps Paul was right, and she had allowed herself to fall under Tate's spell.

She should ring Tate and cancel their outing this morning. It would probably be safer.

She stared at her reflection in the dressing-table mirror. She looked pale and drawn, though her eyes glimmered a deep, bright emerald. She remembered Tate telling her last night that her eyes were beautiful. Hell, she was going to have to cancel, she thought as a wave of panic rose up inside her. Tate was a charmer...a ruthless charmer. To go ahead and see him, feeling as she did, was just asking for trouble.

Hurriedly she rushed out of her bedroom door and down the hall towards the phone. She had just found his number in the book when the doorbell rang.

Helena knew it was Tate even before Mary opened the door and she heard his voice. The deep velvet sound made a shiver of anticipation flood through her body.

She moved out towards the veranda nervously, running a smoothing hand over her hair. She would just have to brazen the situation out, try and remain as aloof as possible.

Then she was face to face with him, and she knew that being cool and aloof was going to be impossible. He looked incredibly attractive in fawn jodhpurs and a blue short-sleeved polo shirt. Their eyes met and he smiled.

She noticed how the warmth of his smile seemed to light his eyes, and suddenly she felt as if going out with Tate for the afternoon was the most wonderful thing in the world.

Barbados had never seemed so beautiful as it did that afternoon. Heat shimmered over the tropical lush green landscape, and the air was fragrant with the scent of sweet flowers.

Being back on Gypsy and galloping across the fields with the breeze blowing her hair back from her face was a wonderfully exhilarating feeling. It was the strangest thing, but she felt alive again for the first time in years.

They slowed to a walking pace when they reached a gate through to a winding narrow country lane. Tate held it for her to precede him through.

She noticed how well he managed the huge black stallion he rode. He was a superb horseman, in perfect control of the highly temperamental animal. When she mentioned this to him he grinned.

'You have a good seat yourself.'

She looked away from the gleam of amusement in his eyes. 'It's a long time since I was on a horse, but, like riding a bicycle, I suppose it's something you never forget.'

'You don't ride in England?'

She laughed at that. 'My life is pretty full with work.'

'But you must get free time?' He closed the gate behind them and they ambled slowly up the road. 'What do you do with yourself—when you're not out on wild dates, that is?'

Helena thought about that for a moment. She was rarely out on any kind of date, let alone a wild one—whatever that might be.

'I bring a lot of paperwork home with me.' Helena shrugged. 'I work out at a local gym, and that's about it.'

'But you like living in London?' He slanted a probing glance across at her.

'Some days I love it.' Her eyes moved across the rolling countryside bathed with bright sunshine. 'Sometimes I'm very homesick.'

There was silence for a while. Perhaps if she were truthful she would say that her days of feeling homesick far outweighed the others.

'Perhaps you should contemplate coming back?'

'I don't know. As I said before, my career prospects are better in London.' She frowned as a sudden thought struck her.

If Cass wasn't here she would be back like a shot. It was hateful to have to admit that to herself, but she could see the truth of it clearly now for the first time. It was very strange, but facing Cass yesterday had somehow unlocked the key to her innermost feelings. She could understand her motivations...her fears...so much better. Perhaps that had something to do with Tate as well...something to do with the way he made her feel.

'What's the matter?' He was quick to notice the expression of consternation on her face, a fact that made her school her expression into a very careful look of bland indifference.

'Nothing.' She leaned forward in her saddle. 'Isn't that St John's Church up ahead?' She knew very well that it was, but she was anxious to turn his attention away from her.

How could she admit to him what had been running through her mind? She could hardly bear to admit it to herself. She sighed and swept her hair back from her face with an impatient hand. How could she have allowed the one person she hated with all her heart to dictate the course of her life? Tate was right. Going to London had been running away.

'Yes, it's St John's,' Tate answered, before turning the conversation smoothly back to where it had been. 'So you wouldn't come back to Barbados under any circumstances?'

'I never said that.' Her green gaze turned towards him. 'I'd just have to have something worth coming back for.'

'Something or somebody?'

The softly asked question made her nerves quiver. What was he getting at? She didn't want him to imagine that she was still in love with Cass, that she would come back for him. The mere notion made her angry.

'Something.' Her voice was unnecessarily harsh. 'I meant a job as good as the one I have in London.'

'I see.' He looked over at her. 'Well, I'm in need of someone to take charge of my accounts department. If you're interested we could talk terms.'

Helena's heart missed a beat. Was he serious? she wondered. That was a fabulous job he was offering out so casually.

She shook her head. 'You haven't even seen my references, my qualifications.' She was totally taken aback. 'Shouldn't you be interviewing for such an important position?'

'I know you're good at your job. Rupert Law was saying as much when I spoke to him at the party last night,' he remarked in a matter-of-fact tone.

'And since when did you pay such close attention to a bank manager?' Helena asked teasingly. 'I thought you didn't have a high regard for them at all.'

'Whatever gave you that idea?' He slanted an eloquent glance across at her. 'There are always exceptions to the rule.' Then he grinned. 'Besides, you seem inordinately fond of being in my office looking through my files...we may as well make it legitimate.'

Her face flooded with colour. 'Come on, Tate...I've apologised for that.' Her heart thundered furiously. 'Is this job offer your idea of a joke? Because if so I don't—'

'I'm not joking, Helena.' He cut across her abruptly and then reached across to take her hand. 'Perhaps teasing you a little...but extremely serious with my offer. Besides, we've sorted out all those fears you had about your father's finances...haven't we?'

'Well...I think so.' She stumbled awkwardly, not knowing what to say. The touch of his hand on hers made her skin tingle. She felt alive when he touched her. All her senses seemed heightened...aroused.

The knowledge made her skin burn with sudden heat. Embarrassed, she pulled her hand away from his. She certainly couldn't think straight when he was touching her.

'The job's yours if you want it,' he told her firmly.

'I don't know what to say.' She took a deep breath, willing herself to think sensibly.

'Don't say anything. Just think about it seriously. We can discuss figures later, and you can compare them to what you earn in London.' Considering the fact that he had just been holding her hand, he now sounded very brisk and businesslike. She just couldn't weigh Tate Ainsley up at all.

If he was offering her a job in his accounts department then surely he had nothing to hide. The thought struck her forcefully. If Tate was dealing crookedly with her father it would show up in his figures for her to find...unless he was damnably clever? Either way, it would be an opportunity for her to try and find out.

She glanced across at him, studying his handsome profile surreptitiously. On the other hand, whispered the voice of caution, working for someone who attracted her as much as he did would have to spell danger. Her thoughts shied away from that emotional direction, but even so she knew she would have to turn down his offer...tempting though it was.

She reined in her horse as they reached the picturesque little church perched high on the hill. It looked for all the world like an English country church, transplanted unexpectedly into a bright tropical landscape.

'It's so beautiful here, so tranquil.' Without being aware of the fact she sighed, her eyes full of longing as they moved over the exquisitely beautiful scene. 'This is one of my most favourite places. I used to come here as a little girl and just walk around the churchyard. I used to dream that I would get married here someday.' The words were softly spoken, her mind deep in memories of her childhood.

'So you didn't always want to be a career girl, then?'

The amused question brought her sharply back to the present, and her face flushed brightly with embarrassed heat. She couldn't believe what she had just said to him...he must think her really silly. 'Well, I was only about nine at the time,' she said defensively.

He laughed, and swung himself off the black stallion. 'Come on, let's go and have a walk around the grounds. Relive some old memories.'

They secured their horses and took the path around the side of the church. It was unmercifully hot now as the sun climbed high in the sky. The churchyard was deserted and silent, the only sounds the call of birds and the soft hum of a small humming bird as it hovered beautifully in front of a pink orchid.

The view from the back of the church was as spectacular as she remembered. Perched eight hundred feet above sea level, the churchyard looked out over a panoramic vista of the Atlantic and the surrounding area of St John.

Helena gazed dreamily out over the deep blue of the sea and the abundant greenery that tumbled down towards it. It was so peaceful, so unspoilt that she sighed. 'This must be one of the most beautiful places to be buried.'

Tate shot her a wry glance. 'I think I preferred your way of thinking at nine...it's the perfect place to get married.'

She smiled wistfully. 'I don't think marriage is for me, Tate.'

'Why not?' He turned to look at her, his gaze raking over the creamy beauty of her skin and the dark luxuriant fall of her hair. 'You are a very beautiful woman.'

'I hardly think marriage has anything to do with looks,' she said with a frown. 'Surely it has more to do with finding the right person—the person whose personality and character complement your own.'

'I quite agree.' He turned away from her for a moment, to glance out to sea. 'True love, I suppose, is a partner who trusts you...who shares your dreams.'

For a moment the tone of Tate's voice threw her. He sounded withdrawn...he sounded sad.

She looked over at him, perplexed. Then, as if becoming suddenly aware of the way she was watching him, he turned back to her and smiled, dispelling the impression of bleakness. His eyes rested on hers as if searching her soul. 'And don't you think that such a person exists?' he asked steadily.

She hesitated, wishing she hadn't embarked on such a personal conversation. How could she tell him that it was her own character that was flawed, that she didn't believe herself capable of embarking on a deep relationship? 'I doubt I would recognise him even if he did,' she said finally with a shrug.

'Perhaps with a little help from the man in question you might learn to recognise him.' Tate smiled gently. 'It's a pretty lonely life on your own.'

'Well, you're on your own.' Helena frowned. 'You're happy, aren't you?'

He hesitated fractionally. Helena couldn't understand this change to his usual jesting, light-hearted manner. 'Yes...I am now.'

The way he was looking at her made her heart jump.

She couldn't understand the conflicting emotions inside her; she couldn't understand the electric undercurrent in the air around them.

'But I don't plan to be on my own forever,' he finished, glancing away from her and back out to sea. 'Not any more.'

That statement sent a strange little quiver racing through Helena. Somehow she had always seen Tate as something of a loner, a man who liked to have affairs but no deep commitments. Why she'd thought of him like that she couldn't say, there was just something about him that suggested he was his own man, that he loved his freedom more than anything else.

'So...have you got a special woman in mind?' She asked the question cautiously, aware that she was probing into very personal areas.

He laughed at that, and linked his arm through hers to turn them back onto the path around the church. 'That,' he said, in a firm unequivocal voice, 'would be telling.'

Was he referring to Antonia? The question lingered at the back of Helena's mind, despite the fact that she told herself very firmly that it was nothing to do with her, and that she didn't really care anyway.

'I think that we might be in for a storm,' Tate observed suddenly as they mounted their horses once more.

She looked up at the sky. It was still a deep cobalt blue, but the trees were very still, she noticed warily. There was no hint of a breeze—in fact, the day suddenly seemed ominously heavy.

'There have been no storm warnings, have there?' she asked with a frown.

Tate shook his head. 'Not for Barbados. But then it

wouldn't be the first time they've got it wrong.' He glanced out to sea. 'I think perhaps we should head back for the castle. It's closer than Beaumont, and I can drive you home.'

Helena nodded in agreement, and they turned their horses around.

At first they didn't hurry, but then, as a breeze seemed to whip up from nowhere, they urged the horses into a gentle canter.

Helena had never known a day to change so quickly. One moment they were baking in hot sunshine, the next the clouds were sweeping in.

They cut across the fields where they could, and as large raindrops started to pelt down on them they increased their speed to a gallop. A parched smell filled the air as the tropical rain hit the dry land, becoming increasingly heavy.

There was something awesome about the power of nature. The wind increased wildly, lashing the rain against their faces, then there was an almighty roar as thunder rent the air.

Helena's heart lurched nervously at the sound, and she was tremendously relieved when they turned up the long drive towards the castle.

They handed the horses to one of the grooms as he dashed out of the stables to greet them. Then they ran towards the front door. The rain was now coming down in continuous sheets, as it could only do in the tropics, and they were both soaked through.

'Wow!' Helena leaned back against the door as she shut it behind her. She was out of breath from the strenuous gallop, and her heart was thundering against her chest. 'I thought the British weather was unpredictable, but that was ridiculous.'

'I think we did the right thing coming here—we wouldn't have made it back to Beaumont.' Tate stepped across towards the windows to look out. 'It's deteriorating rapidly out there.'

Helena moved to stand next to him. The wind was tearing at the palm trees and there was a wild crashing sound as the sea smashed ferociously against the rocks.

'Well, it will probably die down in a little while.' Helena's voice was optimistic, but inside a tingle of nerves started to stir.

'Maybe.' The tone of his voice didn't hold out much hope. 'I think I'll draw the storm shutters across anyway. Perhaps you should ring home, let Lawrence know you're safe here?'

Helena nodded. He was right—her father might be worried about her.

'You can use the phone in here.' He opened the door through to the room they had dined in the other evening. A fire burnt brightly in the grate, sending a warm orange glow over the sudden darkness of the day.

The phone was on a small side-table next to the window. Helena picked up the receiver and dialled her home number as Tate went around securing the windows.

Mary answered the phone. 'Are you all right?' Her voice was panic-stricken. 'They're giving out hurricane warnings on the radio—'

'I'm at Tate's,' Helena cut across her hastily. 'But I—' That was all she managed to say, because the next moment the line had gone dead.

'The line's gone.' Helena looked over at Tate anxiously. 'And apparently they're giving out hurricane warnings!'

Tate nodded. 'One thing's for sure—you won't be able to get home tonight.'

Helena just stared at him for a moment, her heart pumping unmercifully against her chest. 'But…but I can't stay here.'

'Of course you can. I have plenty of room,' he said calmly. 'Meantime, we should get out of these wet clothes. I'll get Joy to run you a bath, otherwise you'll catch a cold—'

'Oh, no, please don't do that,' Helena cut across him. 'I'll dry out just fine here in front of the fire. I'll probably be able to leave in a couple of hours.'

'Don't be silly, Helena. You can't possibly go back out there in this weather.' Tate's voice was calm and totally resolute. 'I'll go and see where Joy is; she can prepare your room for you.'

Then he turned and left her staring after him, her heart beating as wildly as the wind was beating against the walls of the castle.

He was right. She couldn't go back outside—she knew that after one glance from the windows. The trees were bending nearly in half now, and the rain was just torrential.

She sighed. At least they had made it back safe to the castle. If they had headed towards Beaumont they would still be out there now.

Safe… The word hovered tantalisingly at the back of her mind. Was she safe…here alone with Tate?

CHAPTER NINE

THE room Tate showed her into was magnificently furnished. A huge four-poster bed was almost lost in the large splendour of its surroundings. For a moment Helena's gaze was fixed on that bed, and her heart gave a crazy kind of leap. She wondered for the first time if Tate's intentions were honourable. Maybe he hadn't asked her to stay here entirely out of concern for her well being, but out of other much more basic instincts?

As soon as the thought crossed her mind she dismissed it furiously. There was a hurricane blowing outside, for heaven's sake, she told herself fiercely. He could hardly toss her out in such a storm. Even so, she was very relieved when she heard the sound of running water coming from the adjoining bathroom and glimpsed Joy through the partially open door as she ran a bath for her.

'Relax and get out of those wet clothes, then come downstairs and we'll have some dinner together,' Tate suggested easily. He left her then, before she could make the very real excuse that she had nothing to put on in order to come back downstairs.

Joy smiled at her as she came out of the bathroom. 'There's a housecoat hanging behind the door in the bathroom,' she said briskly, as if reading her thoughts. 'If you need anything, please ring the bell next to the bed.'

Helena thanked her, and then as the door closed, leaving her alone, she gratefully slipped out of her wet clothes.

A hot bath helped to relax her, and she was starting to feel a whole lot better about the situation until she put on the white satin housecoat that hung behind the bathroom door.

It felt very sensuous against her skin, and it looked very provocative. Tying the belt tightly around her waist, she looked at herself in the mirror. She looked like a geisha girl—her long dark hair loose around her shoulders, the fine material delicate against her honey-gold skin. Even though she was completely covered up she still wondered about the advisability of going downstairs in what was after all a state of undress.

She was hovering uncertainly between the bed and the door when there was a tap on the door. 'Dinner is ready, Miss Helena,' Joy called cheerfully.

What could she do? Helena wondered frantically. She could hardly put on her wet clothes again.

Taking a deep breath, she opened the door, hoping that Joy would still be out there so that she could ask her opinion on the propriety of her dress. The girl, however, had gone.

Helena's eyes caught on the portrait of Black Jack on the wall opposite. He seemed to be smiling down at her, a devilish gleam in his eye. A shiver of apprehension raced through her.

Immediately she was angry with herself. She was being totally irrational. The housecoat covered her up from head to foot…Tate was hardly going to leap at her with wild, abandoned lust. He could have his pick of women—he didn't need to resort to the kind of tactics she was thinking about.

Resolutely she closed the door behind her and headed downstairs. It was dark now and the castle was lit by oil lamps; they flickered against the white walls, sending shadows dancing across the hall. Outside the wind buffeted against the building, wild and unleashed. It sounded like a howling monster. It was hard to believe that it was only this afternoon that they had ridden across the countryside in such glorious sunshine.

'Helena.' Tate stood up from his chair beside the fire as she walked in. His eyes swept over her figure in the long satin housecoat. 'You look beautiful,' he said softly.

The quietly voiced comment sent a glow of heat spreading through her body.

He was dressed all in black, she noticed. A black open-necked shirt and black jeans, echoing the darkness of his hair. He looked powerfully attractive...too attractive for her peace of mind.

Dinner was a pleasant meal—roast venison followed by strawberries and cream, washed down with a very good bottle of champagne.

'Do you always drink champagne?' Helena asked as he reached across to fill her glass.

'Only on special occasions.'

'Well, we've had it on most occasions we've been together,' Helena said, taking a sip of the frothy bubbles.

'That's because every time we're together *is* a special occasion.' Tate smiled.

A frisson of warning tingled through Helena. So far through dinner the talk had been impersonal—about Barbados, about the weather...she had only just started to relax. She didn't want him to start complimenting her…she didn't want to start getting onto personal ground.

'Have you thought any more about my job offer?' Tate asked suddenly.

She let out her breath in a sigh of relief as he changed the subject towards safer ground.

'I don't know, Tate.' She played with her champagne glass, watching the reflection of the fire catch in its crystal depths. 'I don't think I'm ready to come back to Barbados.'

'Even if I offer to double your present salary?'

The casual offer made her eyebrows rise. 'You don't know what my salary is…don't you think you're being rather hasty?'

He laughed at that. 'You see, already you are looking after my financial interests. No, I think having you on my team would be remarkably sensible. I need a good financial adviser by my side.'

Helena grinned at that. 'Flanneller,' she accused softly. 'You are obviously a born businessman—I bet you've never needed a financial adviser in your life.'

He looked across at her and met the bright green eyes with a directness that made her heart flip wildly. 'Until now,' he said softly, and very seriously.

For a moment she was totally at a loss for words.

He saw the bewildered light in her eyes and smiled. 'I was going to wait until the end of the evening before bringing up the subject of business,' he said gently, 'but I am keen to get it sorted out. I'll pay…' His eyes narrowed as he calculated for a moment, then named a hefty sum that made her eyes widen. He shrugged broad shoulders. 'How about it?'

Nervously her long fingers played with her champagne glass. She was totally at a loss. The last thing she had expected was that Tate would offer her a job this afternoon. Was this the reason he had been paying so much attention to her? Was it nothing to do with pleasing her father?

Her mind was filled with questions. How did his offer of a job fit in with Paul's accusations? Surely there could be no real substance to them...not if Tate was willing to let her comb through his accounts? She felt confused, bewildered. The feeling increased as she met the directness of his gaze.

'I don't know, Tate.' She spoke cautiously. 'It's not really the money that keeps me in London,' she told him quietly.

'So what is it?' He leaned back in his chair, his eyes narrowed on her face in a way that made her feel increasingly vulnerable.

She shrugged. 'Job satisfaction.' Even as she spoke the name of Cass was whirling around in her mind. David Cass was what kept her in London. She knew that now without a shadow of doubt.

'I'm sure you could find that outside the constraints of the bank.' Tate's voice was dry. 'I have numerous concerns that need a very capable hand. I need someone who can work under her own initiative—someone I can trust.'

'How do you know you can trust me?' she asked with a shrug. 'You don't really know anything about my work—or about me, for that matter.'

He smiled at that. 'I know enough.'

'Well, I'm sorry, Tate, but I can't be as decisive as you...' She put down her glass. Part of her was very tempted by his offer, part of her wished he had never made it—had never put her in the position of having to think about everything so deeply.

'I'll just be glad if you will seriously consider it,' he said gently.

How could she not contemplate it seriously? she wondered drily. He was offering very big incentives... But it wasn't the money that tempted her, a little voice insisted, deep down. It was the thought of being with him—he had a powerful magnetism. Despite everything Paul had said...despite her own words of warning and against all odds she felt drawn to him, in a way she had never been drawn to anyone before.

Wasn't that in itself a very good reason to turn down the job? the voice of caution reminded her, as it had this afternoon.

She looked across at him. The light played provocatively over his handsome features and it was hard to tell what was going on behind his cool, watchful eyes. Was his offer based on the fact that she had a top job in London and that Rupert Law had spoken highly of her? Or was it based on other, more shady reasons? She was attracted to Tate...deeply attracted—perhaps in the same way as a child was attracted to fire. It was exciting...but it was dangerous.

'I don't think I can come back to Barbados.' She spoke instinctively, backing away from the risks he presented.

He looked at her quizzically. 'If you don't mind my saying so, you sound as if you're speaking out of emotional judgement, not rational thinking.'

She frowned. 'Why? Because I'm comparing the security of my present job over the temptation of more money?'

'Because you're not thinking about money or security or any of those things,' he said suddenly. 'You're thinking about David Cass. London is your escape route—it stops you facing up to him…up to the past.'

A tremor ran through her body at those words. In a way he was right, only now there was the added complication of the fact that she was attracted to him. She shook her head, not wanting to admit the accuracy of his words. 'You…you don't know the first thing about my feelings…my thoughts.'

'I know more than you think.' He regarded her steadily. 'I know your emotions are very tightly entangled with Cass. Every time I even mention his name your barriers go up and you look emotionally torn.'

She shook her head, her eyes blazing.

'Antonia told me something…after I returned to the party last night, actually. Something about how you and Deborah argued about Cass.'

Helena glared at him. The mention of Antonia's name inflamed her senses even further. 'I can't see what that woman would know about my private affairs,' she said coolly.

Tate shrugged. 'Her words were something to the effect that you were so bitter and jealous about Cass finishing with you that you invented wild stories about him attacking you.' He looked at her hard. 'Apparently Deborah told her that a long time ago.'

Helena stared at him in silence; her heartbeats were so loud that they seemed to fill her ears.

'Would you like to tell me about it?' he asked softly.

'Well, if Antonia's already told you, there isn't much point, is there?' she snapped.

He frowned. 'So it's true…?'

She was consumed with a savage feeling of utter hurt. His opinion of her was obviously pretty low if he could believe such a vicious untruth about her. That knowledge stung, almost as if he had physically slapped her across the face.

'Well, it must be, mustn't it?' she said bitterly. 'I mean, if you've heard it from Antonia…who's heard it from Deborah.'

What was the point of denying it? she thought desolately. He obviously wouldn't believe her anyway. She stood up. She couldn't bear to sit here opposite to him, knowing that he thought such things about her.

'So, now you know the unsavoury details about my past, perhaps you'd better take back your offer of a job. After all, you don't want an unscrupulous trouble-maker on your team…do you? If you displease me I might just be tempted to tell everyone you tried to force yourself on me…mightn't I?'

'Helena!'

He called her back, his voice sharp. But she paid no attention, just hurried from the room as if chased by all the demons of hell.

When she got into her bedroom she leaned back against the door, her heart pumping. Tears misted her eyes so that the bedroom swam before her, a muted mixture of colours in the dim half-light.

Somehow Cass had succeeded in spoiling even the tentative feelings she had started to feel for Tate. He thought she was a woman scorned…the type of woman to make up wicked stories about a man.

'Helena.'

Tate's calm voice from outside the bedroom door made her bite down on her lip.

'Helena, this is just silly…open the door.'

She didn't want to face him, not feeling like she did… She didn't want him to see that he had upset her so much...but if she didn't open the door he would know how much he had hurt her.

Taking a deep breath, she wiped a trembling hand over her eyes and opened the door.

He was standing with an oil lamp held in his hand, spilling out golden light. For a second, though, Helena's attention was caught by the painting behind him. Black Jack Ainsley was holding up a lamp just like Tate's. A warm, welcoming light. Perhaps that was all it had ever been. After all, there had not been a shred of real evidence against Black Jack—just a lot of rumours and speculation.

'Are you all right?' Tate's gentle voice brought her attention winging back to him.

It was a bit late for sensitivity, she thought grimly. He had made it very clear that he believed all the gossip about her.

'Of course.' Her tone was brittle.

'You know, the last thing I want is to upset you, Helena.'

She wished he wouldn't look at her like that—his eyes concerned, sympathetic. He probably thought she was emotionally unstable due to her obsessive love for David Cass. Did the whole island of Barbados think that way about her?

'You haven't upset me.' Her voice was stiff, and her heart felt as if it was pounding into overdrive. 'I think, if you don't mind, I'll just go to bed now. I'm feeling very tired.'

'OK.' Tate's blue eyes moved over her slender frame in the white satin, and she felt herself shiver violently. 'Perhaps you'd better take this light, in case the generator packs up for any reason.'

She nodded. 'Thank you.'

He held out the lamp for her, and she tried to take it without touching his hand in the process. It was probably ridiculous, but she didn't feel she could cope with any contact with him at all.

'I'll see you in the morning, then,' he said easily.

'Yes…' Her breathing felt very uneven as she closed the door on him.

She sighed, and put the lamp down on the bedside table before taking the satin housecoat off and slipping between the white silk sheets in the enormous bed.

She couldn't sleep. The wind was screeching around the castle like a wild banshee, and the oil lamp was sending strange distorted shadows dancing across the walls.

What was Tate playing at? The question danced around and around her mind with the flickering shadows. If he believed her capable of dishonest accusations surely he would never in a million years want her in his employ?

Then again, if Paul's accusations were correct, maybe Tate wanted her to come and work for him for much more devious reasons. Perhaps Tate had doctored his accounts, and had the utmost faith that she would never discover anything untoward. What better cover than to have the daughter of the man you were swindling doing the accounts?

She turned and buried her face into the pillow. She couldn't accept that Tate was so crooked…but then she was looking at him through eyes tinged with emotion. Despite everything, she liked Tate…if she was honest she more than liked him—otherwise his accusations at dinner would never have hurt so much.

She groaned, hating herself for such weakness…such vulnerability. Tate could wrap her around his little finger if he wanted. The situation was explosive—she was heading for disaster if she didn't get a grip on her wayward emotions. That meant going back to London, she told herself fiercely, before it was too late.

The thought of returning to London tore her in two. She hadn't felt as awful as this about leaving Barbados five years ago…but then five years ago she hadn't been in love with Tate Ainsley.

The thought dipped into her mind from nowhere, leaving her rigid with shock. No… She denied those words vehemently. No… She was attracted to him…it wasn't love. How could it be? She didn't even trust the man…not completely. How could you love someone you didn't trust?

Her heart thudded uncomfortably. In that moment she realised that she had fallen hopelessly and irrevocably in love with Tate Ainsley. No matter what he had done…no matter what he thought about her…it was there—a wild, illogical love that burnt so deeply it was painful. It was as if her body accepted a fact that her mind refused to come to terms with.

At some point she must have slipped into a deep and uneasy sleep.

Perhaps it was the sound of the wind outside, but she found herself dreaming of Cass. She imagined it was the same storm raging outside that had raged on the night he had attacked her; she heard his voice, harsh and rasping against her ear; she felt his hands tearing at her clothes…

An almighty crashing sound brought her out of the realms of her nightmare with a suddenness that was disorientating. She couldn't remember where she was, she just knew that she was afraid. That Cass had seemed very close, that danger had seemed to surround her.

The room was cold, and someone was calling her name.

'Helena, are you all right?' There was a loud rapping on the door. Then suddenly it burst open and she sat up, her eyes wide, her breathing laboured.

Tate glanced at her and moved across the room. 'The wind has got the window.'

She followed his movements, noticing that the window catch must have snapped. The noise that had woken her had been the sound of it banging in against the wall. The wind was whipping into the room, tearing at the curtains, making them billow into Tate's face as he struggled to pull the shutters across from the sides of the window.

She hesitated for a moment, watching him struggle. For a few seconds her thoughts were muddled, torn between memories of her wild declaration of love for this man and thoughts of Cass.

Then she reached for the housecoat beside her and slipped it around her naked body. Throwing the covers back, she went to try and help him.

It was very cold close to the window and rain was slanting in with the wind, soaking both of them. Helena held the curtains and watched as Tate pushed the wooden shutters against the powerful force of the wind. It took a few moments, but he finally shut them and pushed the bolts firmly across.

'Hell!' He pushed a hand through dark wet hair. 'I'm sorry about that.'

'It was hardly your fault.' Her breathing was coming

in short gasps, and she was shivering violently from a mixture of cold and the aftermath of shock.

His eyes moved down over her. She realised suddenly that the flimsy white housecoat was barely covering her, and to make matters worse it was almost transparent now that it was wet.

'I'll get you a towel.' Much to her relief, he turned away from her and hurried into the adjoining bathroom.

'Thanks.' She took the pink fluffy bath sheet and wrapped it quickly around herself, hugging its warmth against her shivering body.

'You'd better take your wet things off.' His gaze flicked around the room. 'In fact, you can't sleep in here—this room is too cold now.'

'No…really, I'm fine.' She could hardly speak for shivering, and he flicked her a dry gaze.

'Come on.' With one hand he guided her towards the door, picking up the oil lamp on the way past.

The room he showed her into was much warmer. It was also obviously his room. The covers on the four-poster bed were thrown back as proof of the fact that he had left it moments before, when he'd heard the window break.

He put down the oil lamp on the dresser. 'I'll get you one of my dressing-gowns while you get out of that,' he said briskly as he turned to open doors through to a large walk-in closet. Helena made no move to take anything off. She stood where he had left her, her heart pounding nervously as her eyes stared at the large double bed.

CHAPTER TEN

WHEN Tate came back into the room he had changed the dressing-gown he had been wearing for a black towelling robe.

His eyebrows lifted when he noticed that she hadn't made any move whatsoever to take off her wet things. 'Come on, Helena,' he said, coming across to hand her a thick towelling dressing-gown similar to the one he was wearing.

Did he have anything on underneath that black robe? she wondered nervously, her eyes noting the dark hair on his chest that was just visible at its opening.

'Where are you going to sleep?' she asked stiffly.

His lips curved in an attractive grin. 'Honey, there are fifteen bedrooms in this establishment. The only reason I've brought you in here is because of the fire.' He put a hand on her arm and drew her further into the room, so that she could see the enormous log fire that blazed in the corner. 'I'll take myself off to the bedroom next door.'

'Oh!' She felt a bit foolish for a moment.

'Look, you get out of that wet housecoat and dry yourself off. I'll go down and get you a drink to help warm you.' He held out the robe again, his voice matter-of-fact, his eyes gentle on the pallor of her skin.

She nodded, and accepted the robe gratefully.

It seemed very strange sliding into Tate's bed; it still

felt warm from his body, and as she moved further into it she almost imagined she could smell the faint traces of his cologne, a delicious fresh aroma that for some reason made her heart lurch wildly. Abruptly she closed her mind as she started to remember the way she had been thinking about him earlier...those crazy thoughts of love! It must have been the champagne, she told herself forcibly. But then she had only had two glasses, a little voice reminded her.

Tate arrived back, and held out a china beaker as she propped herself up with pillows.

'Cocoa?' Her eyebrows lifted in surprise as she took the drink from him.

'Beans fresh from the Spice Island—Grenada,' he said with a grin, and then perched himself on the side of the bed. 'Have you ever been there?'

She shook her head. 'I've always wanted to go.'

'You should—it's very beautiful. The soft breezes that blow over it are heady with nutmeg and cinnamon. Dense carpets of tropical rainforests drape the volcanic mountains. It's paradise.'

'Sounds it.' She felt relaxed as she listened to him talking, which was strange because the atmosphere was very intimate, and he was sitting very close to her on the bed.

'If you stay on in Barbados maybe I'll take you there some day.'

She smiled, but it was a smile tinged with sadness. She knew now that she couldn't stay on in Barbados. 'Is that a bribe to make me accept your job offer?' She made her voice as light as possible.

'You've caught me out.' He returned her smile, and for a moment their eyes met and held in a warmly profound moment of communication.

She was the first to look away, her senses reeling, her eyes clouding over as anxious thoughts started to steal back into her mind.

'Why are you offering me this job, Tate?' she asked him huskily.

'I've told you,' he said simply. 'I need someone I can trust…someone who is bright and sharp and will see all the angles. My business in Barbados is expanding very rapidly, very successfully. I need a right-hand person who can keep an eye on everything—someone like you.'

'I see.' It sounded so feasible. And if Tate's businesses were so successful…why would he need to embezzle from her father? 'Things must be going very well for you.' She ventured the words cautiously.

'They are.' There was no doubt in his voice.

'I wondered if perhaps you might have overstretched yourself?'

He shook his head. 'I think you will be pleasantly surprised once you cast that eagle eye of yours over my books.'

She wanted to believe him so much that it hurt.

'And perhaps once you start working for me your father will see some sense and let you take over his accounts as well.'

Her heart leapt at that. Her father's books would give a clearer indication of what was going on. If Tate was happy for her to look at those as well as his own he could have nothing to hide. 'Do you think he would?'

'I don't see why not…especially with combined persuasions from both of us.' Tate's voice was confident. 'Another couple of months and things will get easier for Lawrence anyway—his investments will start to pay off and he'll be altogether more relaxed.'

She put her drink down on the bedside table and glanced up at him, her eyes bright, her heart thudding. 'When you talk about "investments", are you referring to the emerald mine?'

'Yes, I am.' He smiled gently.

'So there is an actual emerald mine?'

He laughed at that. 'Over-brimming with the finest quality gems. You know, you worry too much.'

'I know.' She raked a trembling hand through her hair. Incredibly she felt so much better just for those few reassuring words. It was the first time that Tate had given her a straight answer without getting annoyed, without prevaricating...and it felt good. He sounded so confident, so capable...honest. 'I can't seem to help myself...especially about Pop. He's so overworked at the moment, and—'

'And things will get easier,' Tate said unequivocally. 'He has been overdoing things, I know. Vivian has been worried sick about him as well...that's the reason I insisted on sending Antonia over.'

She felt a surge of relief. Paul had misjudged Tate. All he had been trying to do all along was help. There *was* an emerald mine and her father's investments *would* pay off...very soon by the sounds of it.

Her breath escaped in a sigh. 'But things will get better,' she said gently.

'Of course they will.' Tate's voice lowered suddenly. 'And I'm sorry if I upset you earlier.'

She turned her eyes away from him; she didn't want to think about that conversation at dinner. 'You've already apologised,' she said, her heart slamming uncomfortably against her chest.

'Yes...but it was an inadequate apology. What I said—'

'Tate, I don't want to talk about it,' she cut across him sharply. 'Let's just forget about it.'

'I'd like to.' He reached out a hand to touch the gentle curve of her face. 'But it's not that simple, is it?'

She looked up at him then, her skin tingling from the light touch of his fingertips. An electric feeling seemed to sizzle through her in that instant, and she could hardly drag her eyes away from the magnetising power of those wonderful deep blue eyes. She did love him. The knowledge was emblazoned in her heart...clearly, irrevocably she loved him.

'When Antonia told me about Cass I didn't believe—'

Helena reached out and placed a finger against the softness of his lips. 'I don't want to talk about him,' she whispered softly. 'I don't want to hear his name or even think about him.' She couldn't allow thoughts of David Cass to encroach upon the lovely gentle warmth that was invading her body as she looked into Tate's darkly handsome face.

He reached up and caught hold of her hand. 'Do you know, that's the first time you have voluntarily reached out to touch me?' His voice was a husky whisper.

She nodded wordlessly. And he was the first man she had got this close to without feeling afraid. It was incredible, like being reborn.

'You can't imagine how much better I feel.' She whispered the words impulsively.

One eyebrow lifted. 'About what?' he asked with a smile.

'About why you offered me that job—about my father...about you.' She spoke breathlessly. Her thoughts were disjointed, and clouded with a burning passion that she had never, ever experienced before.

'Good.' For a moment his eyes moved over the delicate beauty of her face. 'Because I need you to stay in Barbados, Helena.'

Her heart skipped and seemed to stop beating. 'Because I'll be good at my job...?'

'Partly.' His voice was silky, low, and his eyes burned into hers with a heat so intense that she could feel herself melting, deliciously dissolving into little pieces. 'But mostly because I want you near me.'

A tremor raced down her body; she felt suddenly weak, languidly hot.

He smiled, and his fingers moved around the side of her face in a gentle caress. 'Do you think it would be all right if I kissed you?' he asked softly, his gaze locked on the trembling softness of her lips.

She felt a wild surge of adrenalin as the blood pumped tempestuously through her veins. Slowly, as if mesmerised, she nodded, waiting breathlessly for the touch of his lips.

Being kissed by Tate was the most delicious sensation—like soft silk against her skin, like gentle sunshine warming her body.

She felt like a flower opening up; she felt free of the dark, torturous images in the deep recesses of her mind that she had associated for so long with the act of lovemaking. Tate was gentle to the point of sweetness, his hands whisper-soft against her body, making her arch nearer, making her yearn for deeper contact.

He was the one to draw back from her. His blue eyes were a deep, almost midnight shade as they stared down at her flushed creamy skin and the softly parted lips.

Was this how Sleeping Beauty had felt when she'd been awoken by her Prince Charming after years of sleeping? she wondered dreamily. She had heard once that the original story had ended with the Prince making mad, passionate love to the newly awakened woman. Helena's face flushed with even more heat at the strange thought.

'Do you think I should leave now?' Tate's voice was a husky rasp, conveying the fact that he was barely in control of his emotions…telling her very clearly that if she wanted to call a halt to this tide of passion she would have to speak now, otherwise they would both be washed away by it…

When Helena woke in the early hours of the morning to find herself wrapped in Tate's warm embrace, she didn't regret her decision one little bit.

She remembered the tantalising feeling of his hands against her breasts, the way she had unfolded beneath him with languid, liquid heat firing her body.

Now, thinking back, it was like riding a dream. It had been a hazy, crazy but very cherished night—a night when she hadn't felt afraid, when she had loved the feel of Tate's body against hers. She had trusted him implicitly not to hurt her, and he hadn't. He had been gentle, considerate and sensuously wonderful.

She sighed and wrapped herself closer to him, studying his face in the early-morning light. A shaft of sunlight lit the jagged scar that ran down one side of his cheek, and she traced it with a gentle finger. Blue eyes the deep colour of the sea opened and gazed into hers.

'Good morning.' A lazy smile tugged at his mouth—a smile that did incredible things to her heartstrings.

'Good morning.' She felt shy for a moment, uncertain of this handsome man who lay naked beside her.

His hand travelled in a light caress down her spine. 'Listen,' he whispered close to her ear, tickling the sensitive skin there.

'Listen to what?' she whispered playfully back.

'Silence.' He smiled at her.

For the first time she realised that the wind had stopped, that the morning sounded calm. 'The storm's abated,' she said quietly.

'Which is strange, because it's still raging in my heart.' He growled the words against her ear in a sudden way that made her laugh, and then he rolled on top of her.

'You're even more beautiful when you laugh...do you know that?' he said, staring down into the soft beauty of her face. 'Even more desirable.'

Her heart turned somersaults as his lips crushed down over hers. Whereas last night he had been utterly tender, this morning his kiss was powerful, his hands firm as they moved over the slender curves of her figure. For a moment...just a moment...she felt herself stiffen. Immediately he stopped.

'Am I hurting you?' His voice was filled with such warm-hearted concern that she felt her body fill with utter desire for him.

'No...' She shook her head.

'It's just that sometimes you look so vulnerable, so scared.' He stroked the tender curve of her face. 'Last night I tried to be as gentle as possible, but I wanted you so much...'

She put a soothing finger over his lips. 'Last night was wonderful,' she assured him, with utter sincerity.

He smiled. 'I'm not looking for points, here,' he said

with a roguish smile. 'It's just that you look so fright-ened sometimes,' he added, kissing the tip of her nose, her eyelids, the soft curve of her lips. 'If I didn't know about David Cass—'

'Don't mention his name.' Helena's voice was un-steady as she cut across him. 'I don't want you to say his name...ever,' she reiterated, a furious gleam in her eyes, an angry catch to her voice. She didn't want thoughts of David Cass to spoil tender moments like these...she couldn't bear it.

His face clouded. 'Oh, I'm sorry, Helena,' he groaned, and cradled her closer against his chest. For a moment there was almost silence, just the beating of their hearts.

Did he still believe that she was in love with Cass...that she had made up those stories? The ques-tion tormented her, but she wouldn't ask. She refused to let Cass spoil these idyllic moments...absolutely re-fused. She didn't want to think about anything except for right here and right now.

Her breath escaped in a sigh, but her body was tense, her heartbeats erratic. She knew he was well aware of the effect the mention of Cass's name had had on her. Desperately she tried to unwind again, to wipe the un-pleasant memories from her brain.

Tate kissed her, gently at first, and she turned into his caress, reaching up towards him. Their lips met in an explosion of smouldering desire. His hands moved over the curves of her body, pressing her against his hard, powerful frame.

She breathed in the scent of him, her eyes open, watching the powerful sweep of emotions playing across his handsome features. She needed to keep her eyes open...needed to know it was Tate who touched her, Tate who breathed passionate words against her ear.

He stroked the smooth curves of her breasts, and they hardened under the skilled seductive caress until she ached for him. When he bent his head and took one nipple into the hot sweetness of his mouth she moaned in ecstasy.

'Tell me you want me.' He whispered the words against her skin, his fingers teasing her, stroking and squeezing seductively while his lips trailed a fiery path from her breast over the flatness of her stomach towards the soft core of her womanhood.

'Tate.' She breathed his name in a wild frenzy, telling him what he wanted to hear, moaning in ecstasy as his other hand stroked up the long length of her legs, his fingers massaging, evocative, teasing, until they moved in between them and her breath caught in a wild gasp of pleasure.

Slowly he stroked her, and like a cat she arched against his hand, inviting more…needing more. She wanted him so badly that she could think of nothing else.

'You have such a beautiful body.' He breathed the words huskily as he moved over her. She felt the hard thrust of him against her and she moved invitingly.

'Darling Helena.' His body moved tormentingly against hers, rubbing over the sensitised areas, causing a sweet flood of desire to overwhelm her completely. His hands took the full weight of her breasts, cupping them firmly as his lips sought and found her nipples.

'Please, Tate.' She moaned the words over and over, almost feverish with desire, the heavy ache inside her growing and growing. She wanted to feel the driving hard force of him, the sweet fulfilment of him inside her. She wanted, she needed as she had never needed anything before. 'Please...please... Love me...love me.'

Their lovemaking was as wild and as uncontrolled as the storm that had raged throughout the night, and then as warm and as sweet as the Caribbean sun. Her body responded and yielded to his domination with utter bliss, utter submission. She was his...she would always be his—no matter what happened tomorrow.

Slowly the ache within her receded, and she lost herself in the tide of emotion, in the joy of loving Tate Ainsley.

CHAPTER ELEVEN

WHEN she awoke from the mists of sleep she was alone in the bed. A smile curved her lips as she stretched languorously. She was in love for the first time in her life and it felt wonderful. Tate was wonderful. She remembered his whispered words of passion last night, and the way he had made love to her again this morning. A sweet rush of tender emotion filled her. She never wanted this feeling to die; she never wanted to be without Tate.

She turned her head and looked around the bedroom for him, but the room was empty. Sunshine flooded through the window, lighting on her clothes hanging on the outside of the closet. Someone had washed and pressed them...

Helena cringed as she wondered if Joy had brought them in here for her. Then she shrugged. What did it matter if Joy knew that they were in love? At this moment Helena wanted the whole world to know.

Stretching, she got out of bed and padded towards the bathroom for a shower. Her body felt slightly stiff from the night of passion, but she had never felt so alive.

For a moment her attention was caught by her reflection in the bathroom mirror. Her skin held a peach glow, and her eyes were glimmering a deep emerald.

She could hardly believe that another human being could make her feel like this.

Did Tate feel the way she did? The question stole into her mind. Did he feel as deeply about her as she felt about him? Had last night been the beginning of a wonderful, loving relationship, or would Tate treat the whole episode in a light-hearted casual manner? He hadn't actually said that he loved her last night.

She tried to dismiss the doubts, but they remained like a shadowy veil over her happiness. With a sigh she turned to take her shower. She would know soon enough what Tate's feelings were; there was no point in worrying now.

About half an hour later she went downstairs looking for Tate, wanting a good-morning kiss, wanting to feel his arms around her again, wanting the reassurance of his smile.

Joy was in the lounge vacuuming. She looked around when Helena entered, and smiled. 'Mr. Ainsley is outside. There has been some damage to the stables and he is seeing to it.'

Helena nodded and thanked the girl.

It was fresh and warm outside. The sky was a perfect blue, as if the rain last night had washed it clean again. Everything felt vital—even the birds seemed to be singing in louder, more melodic tunes than before. Her lips curved in a smile at such a foolish thought.

She found Tate, as Joy had said, around by the stables. He was dressed casually in jeans and a white shirt, with a hat protecting his neck from the fierce rays of the sun as he worked. Part of the stable roof had come off, and he was up hammering it back in place alongside a couple of other men.

'Tate!' She had to call out to get his attention. Her

heart thundered against her breast as she waited to see what reaction she would receive. She felt terribly unsure of this whole situation. Things had moved so quickly last night. Her emotions had undergone such a rapid transformation.

'Well, hello there.' He tipped his hat further back from his face to glance down at her, his smile lazily attractive as his gaze moved over the slender lines of her body in the close-fitting riding gear.

To her delight he put down his tools and came down the ladder.

'Sleep well?' he asked in a low teasing tone as one arm stole around her waist and he leaned closer to kiss her.

She felt herself blush. 'Never better,' she told him huskily.

He grinned. 'Come on, let's get some coffee in the privacy of my study.'

Relief and joy were a heady combination. Tate didn't regret making love to her…he was acting as if he really cared about her.

'Did the storm last night do a lot of damage around the island?' Helena asked anxiously, thinking of Beaumont House.

'No, we've been lucky. I think we just caught the tail of the hurricane.'

Helena nodded, relieved. Hurricanes had wrought some terrible damage to the island in the past. People had been killed, houses blown away. They were lucky it had just been the stable roof that they'd lost last night. The stable roof and her virginity… The crazy thought brought a smile to her face, but then everything seemed to make her want to smile this morning.

They walked in companionable silence back towards the house.

Tate's study was a magnificent room. The walls were lined with books, and a window-seat with views out over the sea made a perfect place for relaxing to read a while.

When Helena remarked on this, Tate laughed and pointed towards the paperwork waiting on the leather-top desk. 'I don't have much time for reading. That's one of the reasons I need you.' He tossed his hat down on the window-seat and raked a hand through the darkness of his hair.

'But only one of the smaller reasons, I hope?' She felt brave enough to venture the question lightly.

'Didn't we go into that thoroughly last night?' he asked in a teasing tone, and then as she blushed he laughed and nodded. 'Oh, yes, Helena...' For a moment his eyes rested on her mouth in a blatantly sensual way—a way that made her have little doubt about that.

With one look he could send her body into total chaos, she thought hazily. 'Well, in that case I would love to take up your offer of a job.' Her voice was slightly breathless as she fought for control of her senses. 'I'll...I'll have to work out my notice in London first, of course.'

He nodded. 'I understand that.' He turned to pour her a coffee from the machine beside him before sitting down behind the desk. 'When do you think you'll be able to start?' he asked, searching through his drawers and taking out a diary.

'Well...' Helena hesitated, the abrupt change from lover to businessman taking her by surprise. 'Say about a month? I'm not sure.'

They were interrupted by a knock on the door, and

Joy popped her head around. 'Antonia Summers is here to see you, sir,' she said brightly. 'Shall I show her in here?'

'Yes, thank you, Joy.'

Antonia drifted in a moment later, looking cool and elegantly beautiful in a cream linen suit teamed with gold accessories. The smile on her face faltered for a second as she took in the fact that Helena was there.

'It's a pleasant surprise to see you so bright and early on a Sunday morning,' Tate said with a grin.

'Well, you said you needed this report typed up in a hurry.' Antonia placed a folder on his desk. 'As I couldn't sleep last night I decided to get it done.'

'That's what I like…initiative and selfless loyalty to the job.' Tate's voice was teasing, yet his expression was serious as he opened the folder and flicked through it. 'You've done good work as usual.'

'Thank you,' Antonia murmured. 'I thought we could go through it point by point today, ready for us to submit tomorrow morning.'

Tate nodded. 'That's good thinking.' He looked up at Helena. 'Would you mind, Helena?' he asked gently. 'It is rather important.'

'No, of course not.' Helena shrugged, and tried to be sensible over this. Tate was a businessman—he probably had deadlines, important deals that just wouldn't wait.

'Good… I'll make it up to you over dinner to-night…how about it?' He looked at her with a raised eyebrow.

She felt her cheeks glow with colour; it was ridiculous that he could make her blush so easily. Tate made her feel like a schoolgirl. She wanted to melt when he looked at her in certain ways...spoke her name with that velvet-smooth seductive tone.

She was going to have to take things slowly, she told herself cautiously. She was going to have to master these new wild emotions until she was sure... absolutely sure about everything.

'Shall I pick you up at eight?' he asked now.

'OK.' She tried to sound casually indifferent. 'Shall I ride Gypsy home? I haven't got any means of transport, don't forget.'

'Oh, I haven't forgotten.' He grinned. 'I'll take you home.'

'I'll take Helena home, if you like,' Antonia offered suddenly. 'That will give you a chance to read through the report on your own first.'

Tate hesitated. For a moment Helena hoped that he was going to refuse, then he looked down at the file again and nodded. 'OK, Antonia, that makes sense.'

Helena tried not to be hurt...she really tried not to care. After all, he had apologised, he had said he would make it up to her. Her heart thudded uncomfortably.

'I'm ready when you are, Helena.' Antonia smiled.

Tate walked out towards the front door with them. As Antonia stepped outside and walked across to her car, Tate caught hold of Helena's arm and held her back.

'You don't mind, do you?' he asked in a low voice, his eyes moving over the vulnerable curve of her lips.

'No...' She hesitated. 'I would have preferred you to take me home, of course, but I understand.'

He bent his head towards her. All of a sudden her body was swept away with the tempestuous feeling of desire as his lips brushed against hers. 'We'll talk tonight,' he promised softly.

Antonia was waiting in the car for her, her fingers drumming impatiently on the steering wheel as Helena climbed in.

'Ready now?' she enquired archly.

'Yes, thank you.' Helena had no sooner fastened her seat belt when the girl took off down the drive with a speed that made Helena look across at her in surprise.

'You and Tate seem to be hitting it off,' Antonia remarked nonchalantly.

'You could say that.' Helena shrugged lightly.

'I know it's none of my business...' The girl hesitated. 'But you know that he has a bit of an eye for the ladies, don't you, Helena? He's a heartbreaker.'

Helena turned wide green eyes on the other woman. She recognised jealousy when she heard it, and that particular emotion was obviously eating Antonia away. 'Come on, Antonia, you and I have known each other for a long time,' Helena said patiently. 'I know you like Tate. There's no point trying to poison my mind against him, because it just won't wash.'

'I'm sorry you feel like that.' Antonia shrugged, not in the slightest bit perturbed. 'Believe it or not, I was only trying to save you some heartbreak...because, believe me, I've been there.'

For a moment Helena was reminded forcibly of the day she had tried to warn Debby about Cass. Debby had thought she was jealous...hadn't given her a chance. Her heart slammed against her chest and she felt suddenly sick. 'What sort of heartache do you mean?' she asked cautiously.

'Paul approached me not so long ago, asking me some pointed questions about Tate's dealings with your father, and asking me specifically about an emerald mine—had I seen any geological reports, that kind of thing.' Antonia looked across at her directly for a moment. 'I didn't tell him anything—at the time I didn't know anything.'

'And what do you know now?' Helena asked with a frown.

'Is this strictly between the two of us?' Antonia slowed the car as the gates of Beaumont House came into sight.

Helena nodded; her mouth suddenly felt dry.

'Well, for one thing Tate owns no such thing as an emerald mine...never has done. I don't know what your father has invested in, but it's not that. The other thing I've discovered—' Antonia broke off and sighed. 'You realise that I'm jeopardising the privileged position I have working for Tate?'

'Yes.' Helena's voice was raw. 'But I won't divulge where I got my information.'

Antonia pulled the car to a halt in front of Beaumont House. 'The other thing I've discovered is that Tate is married...'

'Married!' Helena's heart hammered wildly.

'Years ago, before he came back to live in Barbados, to a girl called Sarah.' Antonia's voice was matter-of-fact. 'I found the marriage certificate among Tate's private files not so long ago.'

'Well...well, where is she now? Has he divorced her?'

'There were no divorce papers in the file. Just a few pictures of her, a newspaper cutting about their wedding...and some first anniversary cards.'

Helena's new-found precious glimpse of happiness crumbled about her in waves of absolute misery. She reached for the doorhandle numbly.

She was in the process of stepping out of the car when the front door opened and Vivian ran out.

Her stepmother's face was drained of colour, and tears were streaming down her face. 'Helena…oh, Helena, thank heavens you're home. I think your father's had a heart attack. I've had to ring for an ambulance.'

She sat in the corridor of a hospital, one of the men

CHAPTER TWELVE

HELENA sat in the corridor of the hospital, clutching
Vivian's hand.

'You do think he's going to be all right...don't you?'
Vivian kept repeating the question over and over, and
Helena kept making the same soothing reply.

'I'm sure he is.' Deep down she wasn't nearly so
confident. She kept seeing Lawrence the way he had
looked when she had rushed into his study—slumped
over his desk, his face a grim shade of white. For one
awful terrifying moment she had thought he was dead.
She shut out that thought; it was too dreadful to contemplate. No, Pop would be all right, she told herself
fiercely...he had to be.

'I wonder where Paul can be?' She glanced at her
watch. It was nearly an hour since she had telephoned
him.

Her eyes locked on the face of her watch. It was
only a few hours since she had lain in Tate's
arms...blissfully happy. It felt like a lifetime ago.

Infuriated by such thoughts, she tightened her mouth
into a grim line. Tate was a charlatan and a rogue. It
was his scheme to swindle Lawrence that had driven
her father to this state. He had placed pressure and
financial worries on Lawrence's shoulders that
shouldn't have been there.

Of course, it was her fault as well, a little voice

reminded her. She should have tackled the problem sooner...should have insisted on looking through his accounts, made him listen to what she had to say. Instead she had sidestepped around the issue, fallen under Tate's spell...refused to believe the truth that Paul had so desperately tried to point out.

The door at the side of them opened, and both Helena and Vivian looked up anxiously, but it was just a nurse walking through.

'I can't stand all this waiting,' Vivian murmured, strain clear in her voice.

'I'm sure it won't be much longer—' Helena stopped abruptly, her eyes locking on the tall, dark-haired man walking down the corridor towards them.

It was Tate Ainsley... She couldn't believe that he had the nerve to show up here. Her heart missed a beat as he came closer and their eyes met.

'I've just heard.' His voice was grim. 'How is he?'

'Tate...oh, Tate!' Vivian got to her feet and rushed into his arms. 'I'm so glad to see you...it's been awful.'

'It's OK, Vivian.' Tate put a soothing arm around her. Watching the easy way Vivian rested against his chest, seeing the comforting arm that held her close filled Helena with a kind of unbearable anguish. For a second...just a second...she too wanted the comfort of Tate's arms, wanted to lean against him and feel the reassurance of his strength. A shudder ran through her as she fought such weakness...this was the man who had caused her father's stress. She hated him, hated him.

He looked across and met the glimmering light of heartache in her eyes. 'Are you OK?' The gentle note in his voice was almost her undoing; she felt like crying. Abruptly she looked away. If only Tate was really the gentle, concerned person that he seemed. If only she could forget the deep need inside her that he had opened up…if only she could forget the fact that she loved him.

Tate frowned as she made no effort to reply. 'Have the doctors said anything about Lawrence's condition?' he asked with concern.

She shook her head. 'They haven't told us anything.' Her voice was stiffly polite. She would have liked to scream at him that this was all his fault, would have liked to tell him to go to hell, but for Vivian's sake she forced herself to maintain a civil front.

'He's been working far too hard,' Vivian said into the silence. 'I should have made him stop…I should have insisted he leave everything until he felt stronger.'

'Vivian, you couldn't have done anything more than you did. Lawrence is his own man,' Tate said soothingly. 'Even if you had locked his office door he'd have found a way to break in.'

Vivian's lips curved in a ghost of a smile. 'Even so… I should have done as you suggested and taken him away on holiday.'

Oh, Tate had played a clever game, Helena thought grimly. Pretending to be so concerned, suggesting holidays, sending his secretary over. No wonder Vivian was totally taken in. Her heart missed a beat… Even now, looking at Tate and knowing the truth, it was hard to believe that he was really so calculating, so hard.

The door behind them opened and the doctor came out. 'Mrs. Beaumont?'

'Yes?' Vivian clung tightly to Tate, her eyes filled with anguish. 'Is…is my husband going to be all right?'

The doctor nodded. 'We'll be keeping him in for a couple of days, as we still have some tests to run on him, but I'm pretty certain that Mr. Beaumont is suffering from no more than chronic fatigue complicated by high blood pressure.'

Vivian's eyes filled with tears of relief. 'Can I see him?'

The doctor hesitated. 'Well, for a few minutes, and only one at a time. He needs rest and he needs peace of mind. It's imperative that he avoids stress.'

Vivian nodded, and with a tremulous smile up at Tate she left them to move in to see her husband.

'Well, that's a relief,' Tate said, moving over towards Helena as the doctor left them alone.

Helena could hardly speak. She was so thankful her father was all right that she was overcome with emotion. For an awful moment when the doctor had come out to see them she had feared the worst. Memories of when she had lost her mother had surfaced with fierce poignancy.

'Helena?' Tate put an arm around her and tried to pull her in against the warmth of his body. 'Come on, honey…he's going to be all right.'

For a second she wanted to melt against him—she wanted to turn to him with a need so strong it made her heart twist over. Somewhere she found the strength to break away. 'Don't…' Her voice broke on a harsh note. 'Don't touch me.'

'Helena?' He looked at her, an expression of genuine puzzlement in his eyes. 'I know you've had a shock, but it's OK—'

'No, it's not OK,' she cut across him, and swung to face him, her eyes blazing. 'It will never be OK between us. This is all your fault. *You* are to blame for my father's illness…*you* are responsible for—'

'Helena, you're not making sense.' He shook his head.

'On the contrary, I'm making perfect sense,' she blazed furiously, her voice a low hiss. All her fear, anger and confusion came rushing out then, in a furious tirade. 'Just because you held me in your arms for one night don't think that it meant something, because it didn't. I hate you, Tate Ainsley…hate and despise you. You have lied and cheated my father. Swindled him out of his money and his land and reduced him to a state of near-collapse.'

Tate's face darkened ominously with every word she uttered. 'And you really believe that, don't you?'

'I more than believe it…I know it to be true.'

'I see.' His eyes moved over her face, lingering on the softness of her lips. The look made her shiver. 'Then there's nothing more to be said.' His tone was quiet, yet it lashed at her like a whip. He turned and walked away.

I don't care, Helena told herself staunchly as she watched him go. I don't care. Then why did she feel as if her heart was breaking in two? she wondered grimly.

It was dark when Vivian and Helena returned home. After leaving the hospital they had driven via Paul's apartment to tell him the good news about Lawrence, but he hadn't been there.

As soon as their taxi pulled up outside the house a dark, shadowy figure detached itself from the building and moved towards them. At first Helena felt her heartbeats quicken, thinking it was Tate, but then as it came closer she saw that it was Paul.

'How is he?' Her brother's face was etched with strain. 'I couldn't come to the hospital, Helena... I felt too damned guilty...too scared.'

'Oh, Paul!' Helena reached to put her arms around him. 'He's all right—just suffering from fatigue and stress...nothing that a little peace and quiet won't heal.'

She could feel her brother shaking against her as he tried to control the sobs that racked his body.

'Come inside, Paul,' Vivian said, putting a gentle hand on his shoulder. 'I think we could all do with a good strong drink.'

He nodded, and silently they made their way inside.

The first thing they saw as they walked into the hallway was the door to Lawrence's study lying wide open as they had left it. The reading light that Lawrence used night and day was still blazing above his desk, and papers were strewn about it, some on the floor the way they had fallen as the ambulancemen had transferred him to a stretcher. The scene spoke of the anguish and speed with which they had left the house.

'Thank God he's all right.' Vivian spoke for all of them.

'I'll tidy up in there while you get us that drink, Vivian,' Helena said in a shaky tone.

Paul followed her into the study, bending to pick up some of the papers as he did so.

'I was worried when you didn't show at the hospital, you know,' Helena said as she started to straighten the desk.

'I know...I'm sorry. I don't seem to be any help at

all around here, even in a crisis. Maybe Pop's right—I need to get my act together.'

'What's with this sudden contrition?' Helena asked with a light smile.

'Well, when I got your message about Pop my immediate feeling was that it was all my fault. I've laid a lot of stress at his door recently, what with my ranting about Tate Ainsley and everything.'

'Yes, well…' Helena didn't want to talk about Tate right at this minute. She didn't think she was strong enough not to break down. She just said quietly, 'Maybe you had a point.'

'There was also the point that you made about my being bitter about my allowance.' Paul looked more than a little shamefaced. 'I know, you see, that it was Tate who recommended to my father that he cut me off for a few months. He said it might help make a man of me.' He gave a self-conscious laugh. 'Hearing that kind of thing about oneself tends to make one feel a mite bitter.'

Helena glanced over at her brother. 'Even so, you were still right about Tate.'

'Was I?' Paul's voice was hollow. 'Afraid not, Helena… I was barking up the wrong tree altogether.'

Helena sat down on her father's chair, her legs feeling weak all of a sudden.

'Rupert Law set me straight, you see, when I confronted him with what he called my "absurd accusations" yesterday.' Paul looked over at Helena when she said nothing. 'You know Rupert, your old boss at the bank?'

Helena nodded. Her heart was thudding so viciously that it was a pain in her chest.

'He told me in no uncertain terms that Tate isn't in

any kind of debt. His finances are extremely healthy. And, are you ready for this?' Paul's lips slanted in a self-deprecating smile. 'The Emerald Mine is the name of a shop…a chain of jewellery shops, to be precise, that Tate owns throughout the Caribbean. They are immensely successful and he has owned them outright for a long time.'

'I see.' Helena's voice was numb.

'I feel such a fool, Helena.' Paul shook his head. 'You remember how suspicious I was when Pop turned down that fabulous offer I got for him on the Bounty Bay land for Tate's smaller offer?'

Could Helena ever forget? It was emblazoned on her mind. She didn't say anything; she couldn't find her voice.

'Well, apparently Tate offered him a partnership in the hotel as part of his deal. It's worth…well, it's worth a fortune. Pop will be a very rich man, thanks to Tate.'

'Tate's been very good to us.'

Vivian's voice from the doorway made them both jump.

'We were in a terrible mess before he made us those offers.' She came forward and put a silver tray of drinks down on the desk. 'You didn't think otherwise…did you, Helena?'

Helena wanted to say no…she wanted to cry. 'I…didn't believe it, not…not really. And then this morning Antonia told me…well, she told me a few things.'

'Well, she certainly knows all about the deal; she's typed up a lot of the contracts.' Vivian handed Helena a glass of brandy. 'Of course, she might just have been hoping to turn you against Tate…' Vivian's lips twisted. 'She must have noticed how close you two are—she was probably hoping to chase you back to London quickly.'

Helena groaned and buried her head in her hands. 'She also told me that Tate was married…I suppose that's a lie as well?'

There was silence in the room for a moment.

'No, Helena… No, that's not a lie.'

Helena looked sharply up at her stepmother, her face etched with sadness.

'Tate was married when he lived in England. He was just twenty years of age, and Sarah Jayne was nineteen. He loved her very much, but she was killed in a car crash.' Vivian paused to take a sip of her brandy.

'It was just after their first wedding anniversary,' she continued in a low, trembling voice. 'Poor Tate was devastated. I think that's why he has driven himself so hard in business and hasn't had any serious relationships with women since. And heaven knows enough women have flung themselves at him. In a way I think he still feels married to Sarah…in his heart.'

For a moment Helena's mind went back to the conversation she had had with Tate at St John's Church. They had talked about marriage…Tate had looked so incredibly sad for a moment. What was it he had said…? 'True love, I suppose, is a partner who trusts you…who shares your dreams.'

A lone tear trickled down the smooth paleness of her skin. 'Oh, Vivian, what have I done?' she whispered in a low, broken tone. 'I love him so much.'

CHAPTER THIRTEEN

A SOFT warm breeze played over the Caribbean, carrying snatches of music as colourful, as intoxicating as the islands themselves.

Helena stood alone on the white sandy beach staring out at the turquoise water. She was oblivious to the music, to the sun beating down unmercifully on her head.

Her mind was on Tate Ainsley, on the fact that she was hopelessly in love with him, on the fact that she had made another major error in her judgement of men.

She was putting off the moment when she would go into the Bounty Bay Hotel and find Tate to apologise, to say goodbye. She knew that her words would probably be useless…that there was no chance of salvaging even friendship from the shattered remains of their brief relationship, but she felt she had to tell him how deeply she regretted her awful suspicions.

It was hard to believe that it was four days since she had spent that glorious night in Tate's arms; it felt more like an eternity ago. Somehow she had managed to get through those days, but it had been hard. Every time the phone had rung she had hoped it would be him…of course it hadn't been. Why would he even want to talk to her after the things she had said?

It had taken every bit of courage to come here to face him, but she felt she owed it to him… She was going back to London tomorrow; she had to see him one last time before she left.

'Helena.'

The quiet voice from behind made her whirl around in surprise.

'Debby!' For a moment Helena moved her eyes beyond the girl, half-afraid that Cass was about to appear as well.

'I'm on my own.'

'Oh.' Helena didn't know what else to say. Her gaze moved over Debby, noticing the pallor of her skin, the uncertain look in her eyes.

'I heard about your father...' she began anxiously.

'He's a lot better. He got out of hospital yesterday,' Helena said awkwardly.

'I'm glad.'

They stared at each other; there seemed nothing else to say. 'Well, it was nice seeing you.' Helena half turned, wanting to get away. Seeing Deborah was painful.

'I wanted to speak to you at the party the other night, but I couldn't work up the nerve.'

The rushed words made Helena stop, and she looked back at her one-time friend with a puzzled expression.

'I want to apologise to you.' Deborah's voice was earnest and low. 'Can't we bury the hatchet, Helena?'

Helena had to swallow hard. 'I'm not sorry for what I said about Cass.'

'No...I didn't expect you to be.' There was a moment's silence. Then suddenly Deborah's eyes filled with tears. 'I made a terrible mistake Helena. I should have believed you when you told me about Cass...but I was so infatuated—' Her voice broke miserably.

Helena's heart lurched with sympathy for her, and

also with a tremendous feeling of relief. Instinctively she reached to put an arm around Debby's shoulder. 'Let's go and have a cool drink and a talk,' she said gently.

They sat at the very edge of the Bounty Bay Hotel terrace, in a private little alcove. The waiter brought them a jug of lemonade and two glasses laced with ice.

Helena listened while Deborah told her how she had made the worst mistake of her life. How at first everything had been very romantic, and then how as time crept on Cass's mood-swings had become more and more noticeable, and finally more and more violent.

'I've been such a fool,' Deborah grated with raw emotion. 'He always apologises afterwards, says it will never happen again…and I find myself believing him.'

'You'll have to finish with him,' Helena said firmly.

'I'm frightened.' Debby whispered the words tremulously. 'Frightened he'll come after me…hurt me.'

Helena's heart thumped painfully. She felt for Deborah; she knew what it was like to be afraid of Cass.

She was quiet while she thought for a moment. It was strange, but for the first time in years she could talk about Cass without any emotion whatsoever…without even a glimmer of hate. The nightmare was over. The grim spectre that had hung over her for so long had died a very real death.

'Go and speak to his mother.'

'Sonia?' Deborah's voice was startled. 'She thinks the world of Cass…she'll never believe me.'

'Oh, yes, she will.' Helena's voice was positive. 'Because she was the one who rescued me that night when Cass…attacked me. Tell Sonia the truth. I think that will be enough for her to do something.'

A shadow fell over the table and the two girls looked up in surprise.

Tate stared down at them, his expression grim as it moved from Deborah to Helena. 'Well, this is a surprise.' His voice held a dry edge.

Helena felt her cheeks burn with colour, and her heart thudded wildly as her eyes met his. 'Hello, Tate.'

There was a tense silence in an atmosphere charged with undercurrents of wild depth.

Deborah shifted uncomfortably. 'I think I'll make a move,' she said shyly.

'Don't go on my account.' Tate's voice was polite.

'No…I have to go anyway.' Deborah smiled across at Helena. 'It's been so good talking to you. I'll ring you soon.'

Helena nodded. 'Do that…and good luck.'

Deborah's departure left even more of a strained silence. Helena looked up into Tate's face, absorbing the rugged contours, trying to ignore the squeezing pain in her heart. She bit down on her lip anxiously. 'I…I'm glad I've bumped into you…'

'Really?' One dark eyebrow lifted sardonically, as if he didn't believe that for a moment.

He wasn't going to make this easy…but then why should he? she thought ruefully. She had said some unforgivable things. For a moment she thought he was going to just walk away, then to her surprise he sat down in the seat just vacated.

'I believe your father is improving?'

'He's much better, thank you. I think he might listen to the doctor's orders a little more in future.' Her answer was stilted. Just talking about her father made her remember the awful things she had said to Tate.

He nodded. 'So all's well that ends well,' he said

sardonically. 'You've even made amends with Deborah, I see.'

'Well…' She shrugged awkwardly. 'I hope so.'

The eyebrow lifted again, then he asked calmly, 'So you've decided to forgive her for not believing you about Cass?'

The casually asked question made her gasp. 'You…you know the truth?'

'Of course.' His lips tightened in a firm line. 'When Antonia told me her little story everything fell into place—the way you seemed so terrified of me at times, the way you hid your feelings behind those barriers you are so good at erecting… I knew then that you had suffered something very traumatic.'

Her face drained of colour. 'I thought you believed Antonia's version of events,' she mumbled incoherently. 'I thought—'

'You do too much thinking—invariably in the wrong direction,' he said with derision.

She raked a trembling hand through the silky length of her hair and looked at him.

'I know… I'm sorry, Tate.' She whispered the words in a husky whisper. 'Really sorry for saying those things to you at the hospital.'

'Which things in particular? That I was a dishonest swindler…or that our night of passion was just a roll in the sack as far as you were concerned?'

Her cheeks flared with colour, and she couldn't look him in the eye. 'I wasn't thinking clearly,' she mumbled. 'I was distraught about my father and…someone had just told me that you weren't all you seemed.'

'Antonia, I presume?' he rasped harshly.

She didn't answer that. There seemed little point now in getting Antonia into trouble with her employer.

That wasn't going to solve anything. 'I know it's not much of an excuse, but I wasn't thinking clearly,' she said lamely. 'My emotions were in turmoil and—'

'And you don't know how to trust a man?' he enquired in a drawling tone.

She looked up into the deep vivid blue of his eyes. For a moment she was reminded forcibly of how he had said that love was having someone who trusted you...someone who shared your dreams. 'Something like that,' she said numbly.

She looked away from him now as she remembered Vivian saying that however many women threw themselves at Tate, he was still married in his heart to Sarah. She had probably been a passing diversion...he probably had no deep feelings for her anyway—she was just another woman falling under his spell. If only it hadn't meant so much to her.

'Anyway, I just wanted to say I was sorry.' She started to move her chair ready to leave; she couldn't bear this any longer.

'So what now?' he asked calmly, before she could get to her feet. 'Running away back to England?'

'I'm going back to my job.' Her voice trembled.

'I offered you a good job here,' he said steadily.

She swallowed hard. 'You can't seriously still think we can work with each other after...after—'

'After our roll in the sack?' he said rawly.

She flinched at those words. That was all it had been to him...but she loved him so much it hurt. Being in his arms had taken her straight to heaven...he had opened up the floodgates of longing and now the pain was unbearable.

'Well...that's the truth of it, isn't it?' Her lips trembled. 'We made a mistake the other night.'

Tate took his time replying to her statement, his eyes moving contemplatively over the sweet oval of her face, lingering on the trembling softness of her lips. 'Would it make any difference if I were to tell you that I don't think it was a mistake?' he said softly.

'Don't, Tate.' She looked sharply away from him. 'Don't try to sweet-talk me or flannel me. I'm not stupid. I think we might as well be honest with each other.'

'I thought I was being honest.' His voice was sardonic, with just an edge of impatience.

'No... Here's the truth.' She looked back at him, her green eyes slicing into him. 'I threw myself at you the other night. You went along with it. It was all a very big mistake.'

'Well, I'm glad you've told me what happened,' he added sarcastically. 'I would have been annoyed if I had missed anything.'

'Sarcasm is the lowest form of wit, you know, and the last resort of a feeble mind.'

'On the contrary, the last resort of a feeble mind is probably trying to understand a woman's emotions,' he said, leaning back in his chair and raking his bright eyes over her creamy countenance. 'You know, when I saw you sitting on my hotel terrace, casually sipping your drink, my first thought was, Hell, she's a brazen woman. She did mean what she said to me at the hospital. She really does hate me.'

She swallowed hard, her breathing shallow as she waited nervously for him to continue.

'Then I sat opposite you and looked at your beautiful face, at the softness of your mouth, the vulnerable light in those emerald eyes, and I thought, No... Helena would never have slept with me the other night if it didn't mean a lot to her…if she wasn't in love with me.'

He watched the flood of colour sweeping into her face with a certain amount of pleasure in his expressive eyes, and the small curve of a smile caught the corners of his sensual mouth. 'Am I right, or am I right?'

For just a second Helena was too astounded by his sheer arrogant gall even to answer that. 'You are a…a conceited…' she spluttered, when at last she could coherently form any words.

'But you do love me?' he continued, as if she had just told him he was amazing and wonderful.

Fear tremored through her. She glared at him through narrowed eyes, trying to ignore how attractive he was, trying to shut out the voices inside her that were screaming yes, yes, yes.

'I…I'm going back to London tomorrow, Tate. I just wanted to say goodbye.' Her voice wobbled precariously. She couldn't voice her love; she was far too terrified of having it flung back in her face. She was far too unsure of herself. She got to her feet and turned blindly away from him.

'Helena, don't run away from me.' His voice, low and steady, stopped her.

She turned slowly and looked at him through eyes that shimmered with tears. She loved him, but he deserved so much more than she was able to give…he deserved total and absolute trust.

'Why didn't you ever tell me that you had been married?' The question just blurted out from nowhere.

His face clouded for just an instant. 'Some things are too painful to even begin to talk about… I hoped maybe you would understand that?'

She nodded, her heart going out to him in that instant, turning somersaults with the need to run into his arms.

She looked deep into his eyes.

He got to his feet with an impatient movement. 'We can't talk here,' he said, coming over and taking hold of her hand. Briskly he led her across the deserted terrace and into the air-conditioned cool of the hotel.

In a daze she noticed that the door he opened was marked 'Private', and then they were in a room that was simply exquisitely beautiful. White leather settees and white carpets were an unobtrusive foil for the green of tropical plants and the blaze of the blue Caribbean Sea shimmering outside the windows.

He turned to face her then, his eyes searching her face with an intensity of feeling.

'Helena, I loved my wife…I have continued to love her even through all these years since her death.'

Her eyes clouded. 'Don't, Tate,' she whispered, her heart aching for him. 'You don't have to tell me.'

'But I do.' He held her shoulders. 'Because until you came back to Barbados I never thought I would feel love again.'

She stared up at him, her heart leaping.

'I love you, Helena… I love you with every beat of my heart. I think I loved you the first time I set eyes on you…I was just too damned foolish to face the truth until you came back to Barbados and I saw you again. Then, that night when you came into my arms so willingly, so sweetly…so trustingly, I knew without a doubt that I loved you with all my heart.'

She swallowed hard on the knot of emotion in her throat.

'You did trust me that night…didn't you?' he whispered huskily.

She nodded. 'Yes...' Her voice trembled with wonder. 'Oh, yes.'

'I know you are afraid of being hurt...' For a moment there was a note of anger in his tone. 'Cass has a lot to answer for... If he ever comes anywhere near you again, I—'

'He's not worth it, Tate.' She placed a soft hand against his lips. 'He's not worth my hate or your anger. I realise that now. It's taken all this time for me to be able to face up to him and the past—to face it and say I wasn't to blame. David Cass is the one who has to live with the spectre of the past, not me.'

Gently he kissed her hand. 'I know I have to take things slowly with you...gently...but believe me, Helena, I would never, ever, willingly or knowingly do anything that would hurt you...'

A tear trickled down her cheek. 'I know...oh, Tate, I know.' She flung herself into the deep, deep comfort of his arms, loving him so much that her whole body ached with it. 'I'm so sorry...' She whispered the words brokenly. 'I'm so, so sorry that I ever doubted you for one moment.'

He kissed the side of her face, and then his lips found hers.

Their kiss was passionately deep and they clung to each other, needing each other more than any words could adequately express.

'I love you, Tate,' she whispered, when at last she pulled away to look up into his eyes.

'Prove it,' he said, an enigmatic look in his deep eyes.

She frowned, wondering what he meant. 'How?'

'Marry me. Come live with me and share my life.'

Her heart skipped a crazy beat and she was totally at a loss for words. 'I… Are you serious?'

He slipped his arms around her waist and pulled her close in against his body. 'I've never been more serious in all my life,' he growled huskily against her ear. 'How about a quiet little service at St John's?'

'I would like that very much.' She whispered the words, her voice not quite steady. 'Am I dreaming, or are you really proposing to me?'

'You're so suspicious.' He kissed her lips with hungry desire, his arms moving around her figure sensuously. 'Now, does this feel like a dream?' he asked gently.

'No…' she sighed, and cuddled closer, needing him. 'No, it feels like paradise.'

He smiled tenderly and wiped a tear away from the side of her face with a gentle finger. 'No more barriers between us?' he asked, in a low, husky voice. 'Because I want you close by my side for evermore. I need you, Helena…I want you more than you could ever know.'

'Only love from now. I promise.'

The world's bestselling romance series.

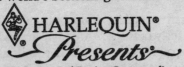

HARLEQUIN®
Presents

Seduction and Passion Guaranteed!

Introducing Jane Porter's exciting new series

THE *Galván Brides*

The Galván men: proud Argentine aristocrats...
who've chosen American rebels as their brides!

IN DANTE'S DEBT
Harlequin Presents #2298

Count Dante Galván was ruthless—and though it broke Daisy's heart she had no alternative but to hand over control of her family's stud farm to him. She was in Dante's debt up to her ears! Daisy knew she was far too ordinary ever to become the count's wife—but could she resist his demands that she repay her dues in his bed?

On sale January 2003

LAZARO'S REVENGE
Harlequin Presents #2304

Lazaro Herrera has vowed revenge on Dante, his half brother, who refuses to acknowledge his existence. When Dante's sister-in-law Zoe arrives in Argentina, it seems the perfect opportunity. But the clash of Zoe's blond and blue-eyed beauty with his own smoldering dark looks creates a sexual force so strong that Lazaro's plan begins to fall apart....

On sale February 2003

Pick up a Harlequin Presents® novel and you will enter a world of spine-tingling passion and provocative, tantalizing romance!

Available wherever Harlequin books are sold.

HARLEQUIN®
Makes any time special ®

Visit us at www.eHarlequin.com

HPGALVAN

$ **Saving Money** $
Has Never Been
This Easy!

Just fill out and send in this form from any October, November and December 2002 books and we will send you a coupon booklet worth a total savings of $20.00 off future purchases of Harlequin and Silhouette books in 2003.

Yes! It's that easy!

**I accept your incredible offer!
Please send me a coupon booklet:**

_____

Name (PLEASE PRINT)

_____

Address   Apt. #

_____

City   State/Prov.   Zip/Postal Code

**In a typical month, how many
Harlequin and Silhouette novels do you read?**

❏ **0-2**   ❏ **3+**

097KJKDNC7   097KJKDNDP

Please send this form to:
    In the U.S.: Harlequin Books, P.O. Box 9071, Buffalo, NY 14269-9071
    In Canada: Harlequin Books, P.O. Box 609, Fort Erie, Ontario L2A 5X3

Allow 4-6 weeks for delivery. Limit one coupon booklet per household. Must be postmarked no later than January 15, 2003.

PHQ402

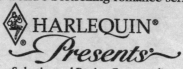

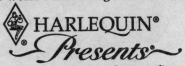

The world's bestselling romance series.